The Sweetest Heist in History

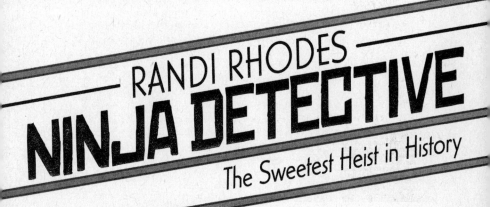

RANDI RHODES
NINJA DETECTIVE

The Sweetest Heist in History

By OCTAVIA SPENCER

Simon & Schuster Books for Young Readers

New York   London   Toronto   Sydney   New Delhi

SIMON & SCHUSTER BOOKS FOR YOUNG READERS
An imprint of Simon & Schuster Children's Publishing Division
1230 Avenue of the Americas, New York, New York 10020
SIMON & SCHUSTER BOOKS FOR YOUNG READERS is a trademark of Simon & Schuster, Inc.
For information about special discounts for bulk purchases, please contact Simon & Schuster
Special Sales at 1-866-506-1949 or business@simonandschuster.com.
The Simon & Schuster Speakers Bureau can bring authors to your live event. For more
information or to book an event, contact the Simon & Schuster Speakers Bureau
at 1-866-248-3049 or visit our website at www.simonspeakers.com.
Book design by Chloë Foglia
The text for this book is set in Janson Text LT Std.
The illustrations for this book are rendered digitally.
Manufactured in the United States of America
0215 FFG
2 4 6 8 10 9 7 5 3 1
Library of Congress Cataloging-in-Publication Data
Spencer, Octavia.
The sweetest heist in history / Octavia Spencer ; illustrations by Vivienne To. — First edition.
pages cm. — (Randi Rhodes, ninja detective ; book 2)
Summary: Randi Rhodes and her friends are heading back to Brooklyn to solve another mystery.
ISBN 978-1-4424-7684-4 (hardcover) — ISBN 978-1-4424-7686-8 (eBook)
[1. Mystery and detective stories. 2. Brooklyn (New York, N.Y.)—Fiction.] I. To, Vivienne,
illustrator. II. Title.
PZ7.S74817Sw 2015
[Fic]—dc23
2014000792

FIRST
EDITION

To all those with dyslexia who continue
to enjoy reading. This is for you!

ALSO BY OCTAVIA SPENCER

Randi Rhodes, Ninja Detective:
The Case of the Time-Capsule Bandit

ACKNOWLEDGMENTS

Thanks to my family, all of my nieces and nephews, and my team who made it possible: Andy McNicol, Brian Clisham, Brad Slater, Melissa Kates, Bria Schreiber, Karl Austen, Paul Crichton, and Zareen Jaffery.

The Sweetest Heist in History

CHAPTER ONE

THE HEIST

Randi Rhodes pressed a button on her walkie-talkie and whispered into the receiver, "Target is approaching from due south, heading in the direction of the Deer Creek Bank. Ninja Two, can you make a visual ID?"

"Negative, Ninja One," came D.C. Cruz's hushed reply. "Target is wearing a hat and sunglasses. And how 'bout that— sparkly purple sneakers. Looks like a female to me."

Randi ran through a list of suspects in her head. None of them would be caught dead in purple sneakers. The shoes had to be part of the thief's disguise.

"This is Ninja Three. Target just entered the alley next to the bank," Pudge Taylor reported.

"Let's give her a minute and then move in at exactly"—Randi checked the watch on her wrist. She never allowed cell phones on stakeouts. They had a way of ringing or lighting up at the very worst moments. So the three ninjas wore watches, and their timepieces were perfectly synchronized—"six fifty-two," she ordered.

"Roger that," her colleagues replied in unison.

Randi took the opportunity to check Founders' Square for other signs of activity. It was a flat, grassy park in the center of sleepy Deer Creek, Tennessee. In the fall and winter, when the tourists who came to Deer Creek for the fishing were gone, the stores surrounding the square closed up early. That night in Founders' Square, only the bakery was still serving customers. There was no one in the park who might interfere with the ninjas' operation.

Randi sat back on her haunches and grinned. Dressed in black from head to toe, she was all but invisible in the dark. Anyone strolling through Founders' Square would never have spotted her crouched behind the monument in the center of the park. Her pulse was racing, and despite the chill in the air, her palms were sweating. Randi hadn't felt so alive since the previous summer, when the ninja detectives had solved their first case together.

That's right, she thought. *Let's show them that the last case wasn't a fluke. The world's greatest crime-fighting team lives right here in the middle of nowhere. And we're not going to let this town forget it.*

It had been five months since Randi and her father had sold their house in Brooklyn, New York, and moved to Deer Creek, Tennessee. Her first summer in the mountains had been unexpectedly thrilling. Randi had made two new best friends, formed the crime-fighting Ninja Detectives Club, and solved the Case of the Time-Capsule Bandit. But the excitement had come to an abrupt end with the start of school. Since August, she and her fellow ninja detectives, D.C. Cruz and Pudge Taylor, had been forced to take a series of second-rate cases. In September, they'd wrangled a rogue opossum that was terrorizing the sheriff's pet chickens. Then they'd collared a third-grade graffiti artist who enjoyed drawing unflattering portraits of fifth graders on the bathroom stalls at school. At the end of October, Randi and her team had investigated a series of jack-o'-lantern squashings. That case had seemed quite promising at first. Randi had hoped that the vandalism might be the work of teenage thugs or Halloween haters. But the culprit had turned out to be an ordinary bear that had wandered out of the woods one night with a hankering for half-rotten pumpkin.

By the middle of November, Randi was worried that her detective skills would end up wasted in a town like Deer Creek. She'd lost all hope of investigating anything truly criminal. Then, finally, a week before Thanksgiving, Randi's prayers had been answered. The Deer Creek Bank had been robbed.

She'd heard about the crime the usual way—by eavesdropping on the sheriff. Deer Creek didn't have a newspaper or television station. But when anything happened, you could always depend on the town's two biggest gossips, Sheriff Ogle and Betty Prufrock, to get the word out. Randi had been grabbing a treat at Betty Prufrock's ice cream parlor when she overheard the sheriff, Mayor Landers, and Mrs. Prufrock discussing the

theft over double-scoop cones. From what Randi could gather, someone had slipped into the Deer Creek Bank after office hours. The thief never touched the money in the vault or the tills. Their loot of choice was office supplies—and they'd gone straight for the good stuff. The rubber bands and paper clips had remained untouched. Instead, the burglar had taken Post-its and Sharpies, notebooks and highlighter pens.

It had to be one of the employees, Randi had heard the sheriff say. The culprit in question knew how to turn off the alarms and slink around the security cameras. The bank's new owner was demanding the sheriff set up a stakeout. But the sheriff seemed convinced that the crime was a one-time affair.

"Who's gonna use that many office supplies?" she'd asked her friends.

"Maybe a burglar with a lot of pen pals?" Betty Prufrock had suggested.

The mayor, who was sitting with his pet skunk curled up in his lap, shook his head at the question and wondered out loud if the world had gone totally nuts.

Randi had a hunch that the thief wasn't done with the Deer Creek Bank. The stolen office supplies were likely being sold online. And Post-its didn't come cheap. The crook was probably making a killing. And he (or she) must have figured out that the sheriff wasn't interested in investigating stolen highlighter pens.

Pudge had spotted an office supply delivery truck parked in front of the bank that morning. A little afternoon sleuthing had confirmed that the supply closet had been restocked. If Randi was right, the thief would soon be going back for more.

"Ninja Two and Ninja Three, get ready to rock and roll," Randi whispered into her walkie-talkie. The time had come to crack the case.

"Ninja One, we have a problem," Pudge replied. Randi heard a high-pitched giggle in the background, and she knew Pudge's cover had been blown.

Randi peeked over the monument. Pudge was right where she'd left him—stationed behind a car parked on the east side of the square. But he was no longer alone. Two little girls in cotton-candy-colored coats had ambushed him. Randi recognized Pudge's eight-year-old twin sisters, Maya and Laeleah, who appeared to be experiencing mind-bending sugar highs. One of the girls had nabbed Pudge's hat while the other was trying to climb her brother for a piggyback ride. The frenzy had attracted the attention of a tall, well-dressed woman who'd just exited the Founders' Square Bakery with a cake box in one hand. Pudge's mom must have taken the girls out for dessert.

"Kelly Eugene Taylor, is that you?" she asked, using the name Pudge always begged her not to mention in public. "Why on earth are you hiding behind that car? And why weren't you home when dinner was served? Your father is *not* a happy man right now."

"But, Mom . . ." Pudge tried to get a word in edgewise.

"Don't *but, Mom* me, mister. Get your rump off the pavement and help me get these two girls home. I swear all it takes is a packet of sugar to turn them stark raving mad."

"But, *Mom!*" Pudge tried again.

"*Now*, Pudge!" his mother ordered in a voice that was pure business.

Randi felt for the kid; she really did. But she couldn't allow Pudge's capture to compromise the entire mission. She pressed the button on her walkie-talkie.

"Ninja Three, we're going in without you."

"Awww, do you have to?" Pudge groaned just before Randi switched off her walkie-talkie.

She crept through the dark park toward the alley that ran down the right side of the bank. D.C. was already waiting for her in the shadows.

"Look," D.C. whispered. The side door of the bank was ajar. They had planned to ambush the thief in the alley, but the opportunity before them was too good to resist. They could get inside the bank and capture the culprit red-handed.

Together Randi and D.C. tiptoed through the dark bank toward a dim light at the far end of a hall. As they drew closer, they could hear office supplies being tossed into a sack. Then, at last, they could see the bandit. She couldn't have been more than five foot two, and she was wearing a black designer sweat suit. A swatch of dyed blond hair stuck out from beneath a black knit hat with a fuzzy pom-pom on top. When D.C. gasped, the thief spun around at the sound. Even with sunglasses hiding most of the girl's face, Randi had no trouble identifying the criminal. It took every ounce of restraint Randi could muster to keep from hopping up and down and squealing with sheer delight.

It was better than opening the best present on Christmas morning. It was more thrilling than the brightest fireworks display on the Fourth of July. The person raiding the supply closet was none other than Randi Rhodes's archenemy Amber-Grace Sutton, daughter of the Deer Creek Bank's former owner. Her father, Dean Sutton, had been forced to sell the bank after the ninja detectives had exposed him as a traitor and a crook. For months, Amber-Grace had been looking for a way to settle the score with Randi, D.C., and Pudge.

The flash of a camera lit the scene. D.C. had snapped a picture of the teenage robber holding a fistful of Post-its and a bagful of loot.

"Bus-*ted*," Randi sang.

Amber-Grace dropped the stolen goods and hurled her body toward the exit. But it was too late. Randi swung the door of the supply closet shut, trapping the other girl inside.

"Let me out of this closet, you motherless Yankee, or I'll turn everyone at school against you! I'll have my boyfriend . . ."

As Amber-Grace shouted insults and threats and pounded on the door, Randi Rhodes whipped out her cell phone and dialed the Deer Creek Police.

~ ~ ~ ~

When Sheriff Ogle answered, Randi instantly knew that something was off. The sheriff didn't seem surprised to be hearing from Randi. Of course, the bank heist wasn't the first Deer Creek crime that the ninja detectives had solved, but Randi expected the sheriff to sound a bit more shocked when she heard the reason for Randi's call. Instead, she said, "Thanks a bunch for the tip, Miranda. I'll be right over."

There weren't any sirens when Sheriff Ogle arrived fifteen minutes later. The police station was only a few blocks from the bank. She had walked to the scene of the crime. With her big down coat on, Sheriff Ogle looked a bit like a bowling ball. She was chewing on a doughnut that she'd stopped off to pick up from the bakery.

"Good work, you two," the sheriff announced, panting from the walk. "Let's see what we got here."

She swallowed the last bite of her doughnut, took a deep breath, and threw open the door of the supply closet. There, sitting on the floor, was a thirteen-year-old girl in a black sweat suit and purple sneakers. Her swag bag had been emptied and its contents were now back in neat stacks on the shelf. Amber-Grace's black hat and sunglasses were nowhere to be seen.

"Those two brats locked me inside this closet!" she wailed, crocodile tears streaming from her eyes.

Then a man's booming voice came from behind Randi. "Amber-Grace, is that you? What in the sam hill is going on?"

Randi spun around to see Dean Sutton charging down the corridor. He hadn't worked at the bank in months. There was no reason for him to be at the scene of the crime—unless the sheriff had called him.

Randi peered up at the sheriff, who once again showed no sign of surprise. She'd been expecting Dean Sutton to arrive. Whatever was going on, the sheriff was behind it.

"I think maybe your daughter should answer that," Sheriff Ogle told him. "Looks to me like she might have been doing some shopping."

Dean Sutton's voice softened. "Amber-Grace, honey, what on earth are you doing in there?" He spoke to his daughter like she was a testy toddler or a prize poodle.

"I was just picking up a few supplies for an art project," the girl said, sobbing. "I wanted to make Mama a surprise gift for Thanksgiving, and you never give me money to buy anything anymore."

Randi couldn't help but laugh. "You were going to make a gift for your mom out of Post-its and binder clips? I had no idea you were still in kindergarten."

"I don't think that kind of nastiness is necessary," Dean Sutton snipped.

"It's okay. I don't listen to her, Daddy," Amber-Grace whined. "Randi's just jealous. She only says mean things because her own mama is dead."

The last word hit Randi like a slap in the face. She could feel her fists tightening into two solid balls. Randi had been itching to show Amber-Grace a few of her latest Tae Kwon Do moves, and it was starting to seem like the perfect time.

D.C. grabbed Randi's arm. "Don't do it. Empty your mind," he whispered in her ear, quoting the ninja detectives' hero, the Kung Fu master Bruce Lee. "Be formless. Shapeless. Like water."

Randi closed her eyes and tried to take his advice. But a punch or two would have made her feel a lot better.

"Well, I think this is about all the excitement I can handle in one night," the sheriff announced. "Mr. Sutton, why don't you go on and escort Amber-Grace home."

"I refuse to leave before charges are pressed," Dean Sutton said.

"I'm not pressing charges. I'm sure Amber-Grace will return everything that she's taken," the sheriff replied. "As soon as she's done making that gift for her mama." Even Sheriff Ogle was having a hard time keeping a straight face about that one.

"I'm not talking about Amber-Grace!" Dean Sutton bellowed again. "These two delinquents just had my daughter locked in a closet! Isn't that what you'd call kidnapping?"

"No, sir," Sheriff Ogle said. "Technically, that would be false imprisonment. But maybe we should check the security tapes to find out how your daughter ended up in the closet. By the way, I've been meaning to ask you, Dean. How do you suppose Amber-Grace got inside the bank in the first place? I haven't done any investigating yet, but I reckon she must have used a key. You don't happen to have any old keys to the bank lying around, do you, Dean? The new owner was pretty sure you were supposed to have handed all your keys over."

Dean Sutton's face turned a bright, blazing red. There was no mistaking what the sheriff was trying to say. His daughter had broken into the bank using keys he wasn't supposed to have.

"Get up!" he growled at his daughter. "We're leaving."

"But, Daddy!" Amber-Grace wailed.

"Don't make me say it twice," Dean Sutton warned through clenched teeth. He grabbed his daughter's hand and yanked her to her feet.

"Don't forget to drop those keys off at my office on your way home," Sheriff Ogle called out as the Suttons hurried out the door. "I don't think Amber-Grace needs to be doing any more art projects, do you?"

"You knew all along, didn't you?" Randi asked the sheriff as soon as the Suttons were gone.

"Knew what?" Sheriff Ogle pulled a grease-spotted bag out of her coat pocket. Inside was another doughnut.

"That Amber-Grace was the thief," Randi said. "You just wanted us to do the work and catch her for you. This was a setup from the very start, wasn't it?"

"I'm afraid that's OPB," Sheriff Ogle replied with a frown.

"That stands for official police business. But a *setup*? That's not a very nice way of putting it, Miranda. I just thought it could save everyone a lot of trouble if the law-enforcement community didn't get too involved. Amber-Grace may be a brat, but she's been through a rough time lately. She doesn't need to get arrested on top of it."

Amber-Grace had been through a lot? Randi thought miserably. Had Amber-Grace lost her mother? Or been dragged to a tiny town a thousand miles away from her home?

"You two better skedaddle," the sheriff said with a mouth full of doughnut. "It's eight o'clock, and I bet you both missed dinner. Wouldn't want y'all to go to bed on an empty stomach." ☠

———

☠ Go to Appendix A to complete the Ninja Task!

CHAPTER TWO

FROM BAD TO WORSE

What would Glenn Street do? Randi asked herself as she pedaled down the gravel road that ran beside the river and led to her house. Glenn Street was the heroine of the world-famous detective novels that her dad, Herb Rhodes, once wrote. She was a karate-kicking, wisecracking private eye—and everything Randi dreamed of being. Glenn Street was the one who'd inspired Randi to become a detective. Randi had taken on her first case the same day she'd finished her first Glenn Street novel. A band of delinquents had been smashing car windows in her old neighborhood in Brooklyn. Randi had filmed them in action—and then anonymously e-mailed the video to the police.

What would Glenn Street do? As much as she hated to admit it, Randi knew that the answer was obvious. Glenn Street would never in a million years set foot in a place like Deer Creek, Tennessee.

Fortunately, there was a single ray of sunshine breaking

through Randi's dark mood. It was Saturday night, and Thanksgiving break would begin on Tuesday. That's when she and her dad were heading to Brooklyn. Randi's aunt Gigi had been working overseas for the past year. But now she was back in New York, and she had invited the Rhodes family to stay with her over the long weekend. Randi had been looking forward to the trip for months. Her mother's younger sister, Gigi, was fun, energetic, and just a little bit crazy—the perfect aunt, in other words. She'd already promised to take Randi to visit the dinosaurs at the Museum of Natural History, the mummies at the Brooklyn Museum, and the criminals at the Museum of the American Gangster.

But the trip wasn't just a holiday for Randi. Brooklyn was where her mother was buried, and it had been almost six months since Randi had visited her grave. She had so much to tell her mom. About her new life and new friends. About the cases she'd solved and the Miss Catfish crown that she'd won. Randi wished more than anything that she could have one last afternoon with her mom. She daydreamed about walking past the old house on Bergen Street and finding her mother waiting on the stoop to greet her. Sometimes Randi missed her so badly that her whole body hurt.

Randi hit the brakes at the end of her driveway, sending a spray of gravel into the bushes. The lights in the house were blazing.

Randi checked her watch. It was almost eight thirty. She was exactly two hours late for dinner. As she climbed the stairs to the front door, she prepared herself for the lecture she was bound to receive.

"There you are!" Mei-Ling called out with a smile when Randi stepped through the door. She was a small woman in her early seventies with long silver hair. Mei-Ling might have had a gentle manner and a charming Chinese accent, but Randi knew she could be tough as nails. She had come to stay with the Rhodeses after they'd moved to Deer Creek. Now she was part of the family. Mei-Ling was in charge of the house. And when she cooked one of her fabulous meals, she expected both Rhodeses to be home on time to enjoy it.

"I'm making your favorite—catfish dumplings!" Mei-Ling bustled back to the stove and began dishing dumplings from a pan.

"You guys haven't eaten yet?" Randi asked. Something very strange was going on.

"We've been waiting for you." Randi's dad had emerged from his study. He gave his daughter a peck on the top of her head.

Randi stared up at her father. She might have inherited her mom's curly red hair, but she'd gotten everything else from her dad. They were both tall and lanky, with expressive faces that made it hard for them to conceal their feelings. And

Randi could tell that her father had something he was trying to hide.

"Everything okay here?" she asked cautiously.

"What do you mean?" Herb asked innocently as he chose a chair at the table. "Of course everything's okay! Have a seat. You must be starving."

Randi plopped down in a seat opposite her father's. "You're acting kinda weird. Are you sure this isn't about the bank heist?"

"Bank heist?" her father asked with one eyebrow raised. "I thought you were going to try to stay out of trouble."

"I don't have any choice," Randi grumbled. "I've been looking all over for it, but there's no place to *find* trouble in this Podunk town."

Herb Rhodes would usually defend Deer Creek to the death. But this time, he chose not to argue. That's when Randi began to get nervous. Then Mei-Ling joined them at the table and kept her eyes on the dumplings she was serving the three of them. Something had happened. Her father and Mei-Ling both knew what it was.

Randi pushed her plate back. "Okay, spill it, you two," she demanded. "Tell me the big secret right now or I'm going on a hunger strike."

"Great. That will leave more dumplings for the rest of us," Herb joked weakly.

"Come on, Dad," Randi prodded.

Herb set his fork down. "Okay. You know how the new book is doing unexpectedly well?"

Randi nodded. Her father's latest novel wasn't even in stores yet and it was already the hottest book around. Readers were thrilled that the author of the Glenn Street books had finally written a novel for young people. And it didn't hurt that *The Ninja Detectives* was rumored to be based on a true story.

"It's doing so well that my publisher wants me to go on tour."

"That's fantastic!" Randi exclaimed. She'd been expecting terrible news.

"Starting on Tuesday," Herb added.

"Wait. *This* Tuesday?" Randi asked.

"Yes," Herb confirmed.

"No. No, you can't!" Randi said. She could already hear a note of desperation creeping into her voice. "It's Thanksgiving. We're going to Brooklyn, remember? You've got to tell them that the tour has to wait—or that you won't be able to make it."

"Randi." Her father leaned across the table and tried to take her hand, but she jerked it away before he was able. "Work with me on this one, kiddo. You're the one who convinced me to come out of retirement. Now that I'm a writer again, going on book tours is a big part of the job. My publisher says this one is very important. I can't tell them no."

Randi balled her napkin up in her fist. "You can't say no to *them*, but you're happy to say no to *me*. I've been waiting for this trip for months. But that doesn't matter to you, does it?"

"Of course it does!" Herb said. "We can try to make it up North for Christmas."

"*Try?*" Randi spat.

Herb hung his head. "I can't make any promises. I have a responsibility to my readers."

"Randi." Mei-Ling's voice usually soothed her, but this time she could feel the tears coming, and she needed to leave before they started to fall.

Randi threw her napkin down on the table and stood up, pushing her chair back so violently that it almost toppled over.

"I thought you'd changed," she told her father. Then she stomped up the stairs to her room.

Almost two years had passed since her mother's death, and Randi and her dad were right back where they'd started. When Randi was little, her father had often seemed more like a favorite guest than a regular dad. He was always off on one book tour or another. In those days, Randi hadn't minded much. She'd had her mom, after all. And they'd always stayed busy while her dad was away. There were always parks to explore and brownies to bake and school projects to finish. Then one day Randi's world had crashed down around her.

Herb Rhodes had been on a book tour in Europe when

they'd found out that Randi's mom was sick. He'd sworn he would never leave his family behind again. Now Randi was all that was left of his family. They'd moved to Deer Creek to live a simpler life. Not even six months had passed and the famous Herb Rhodes had already broken his promise.

There was a knock at the door. "Randi?" Mei-Ling poked her head inside.

Randi buried her head in a pillow. She could hear Mei-Ling set a plate down on her dresser. As miserable as she was, the smell of catfish dumplings made Randi's mouth water.

"Go away," Randi grumbled.

She felt Mei-Ling sit down on the bed. She expected a lecture or a pep talk, but Mei-Ling held her tongue. Instead, she rubbed Randi's back while the tears soaked her pillow.

"You know what's funny?" Randi asked through her sobs.

"What?" Mei-Ling replied in her steady, soothing voice.

"Dad once told me that my mom was his inspiration for the Glenn Street books, and I figured he was just making stuff up. I mean, if he thought my mom was so interesting, why didn't he try to spend more time with her?"

"I think Herb wonders about that too," Mei-Ling confided. "I suspect he might act differently if he had the chance to live those years over again."

"You sure? 'Cause now he's doing the same thing to me that he did to her."

"What do you mean?" Mei-Ling asked.

"Don't you see? That stupid book he just wrote is about *me*. That's what Herb Rhodes does, Mei-Ling. He sticks people in novels so he doesn't have to deal with them. I'm not really his daughter anymore. I'm just another one of his characters now."

CHAPTER THREE

DOUBLE TROUBLE

Randi was up at the crack of dawn. It wasn't even seven o'clock when she hopped on her bike and headed for the hideout. A frost had visited the mountains, and the grass along the road sparkled in the morning light. She could hear the river burbling beside her and a crow cawing overhead. She pedaled down the center of the road, knowing she wouldn't pass a car the entire ride. It was Sunday morning, and the town of Deer Creek was fast asleep.

The ninja detectives' hideout and official headquarters was located in a shack behind D.C.'s house on the edge of Guyton Orchard. In the summer, the little building was hard to spot among the apple trees. But the orchard's leaves had fallen in early October. Now that winter was creeping closer, the hideout was no longer hidden.

The padlock on the door caught Randi's eye before she hopped off her bike. It was open and dangling from the door like a one-armed monkey. Someone was inside. A few months back, it wouldn't have mattered. The only things a thief would have found inside the shack were Bruce Lee posters and empty Capri Sun pouches. But the town of Deer Creek had been generous after the kids had saved the founders' treasure. Now each of them had a state-of-the-art computer and all the detective tools they could want. They kept most of their new equipment locked up in the hideout.

Randi tiptoed to the door of the shack. As long as the intruder wasn't armed, she had the advantage. There wasn't anyone in Deer Creek, Tennessee, who could match her Tae Kwon Do skills.

"Freeze!" she shouted, throwing the door open so hard that it slammed against the side of the shed.

The person inside screamed. A carton flew in the air, flinging chocolate milk across the room.

"Randi!" Pudge yelped. "You nearly scared me to death! What are you doing here so early?"

Randi put her fists down and waited until her heart was thumping at a normal speed. "What am *I* doing here? What are *you* doing here?" she demanded.

Pudge picked up a roll of paper towels and began sopping up the chocolate milk. "I got up early and sneaked out of the house before my dad could give me any chores. After last night, I needed some peace and quiet," he said. "I can't believe my bratty sisters nearly screwed up our surveillance."

"It's okay," Randi replied, dropping down into a beanbag

chair. "Turns out it was a big setup anyway. Did D.C. tell you who the thief was?"

"Amber-Grace. He said the sheriff let her off the hook, too. Guess justice wasn't served."

"You can say that again," Randi grumbled. "This town is a detective's nightmare. I can't believe we both have to live here."

"Well, at least you have your trip to Brooklyn to look forward to," Pudge said, trying to cheer her up.

"Not anymore," Randi said. "My dad decided he'd rather go on a book tour. I'm staying here for the holiday."

"Oh." Pudge grimaced. "That stinks. But at least you won't be trapped in a minivan with three screaming girls for fourteen hours."

Pudge and his entire family were going up North to spend Thanksgiving with their grandmother.

"Is that how long it takes to get to Boston?" Randi asked.

"If we're lucky," Pudge said. "Depends on how many bathroom breaks and food stops we make on the way. My dad won't let anyone eat in the car, so it takes a million years to get anywhere. The whole ride is going to be painful. Whenever we go on a trip, my dad always puts me in charge of Maya, Laeleah, and Sasha. I'm supposed to make sure they don't get in trouble. Then they do, and I'm the one who gets yelled at."

"At least your dad cares enough to get mad at you." D.C. pushed through the door and into the hideout. He was wearing a black martial arts uniform called a *dobok*, which Randi had given him. He'd grown since he'd gotten it, and there were a few inches of bare skin between the hem of his pants and the top of his shoes. As usual, D.C.'s messy black hair was held back by a yellow Tae Kwon Do belt. The rims of his eyes were red, and two of his knuckles were scraped up. When D.C. got mad, he liked to put on his *dobok* and punch apple trees.

"Uh-oh," Pudge muttered under his breath. The signs were unmistakable. Something truly terrible had happened.

Randi stayed silent, but she felt her stomach twist into a knot. D.C. had been talking about his dad nonstop for a month. He hadn't seen his father in years—not since his parents had divorced when he was in the fourth grade. But in early October, he'd gotten an unexpected phone call. His dad was driving down to Tennessee around Thanksgiving. He wanted to visit the orchard to see his boy.

D.C. had immediately begun preparing for the visit, and his friends had pitched in to help. Windows that hadn't seen a rag in years were washed until they sparkled. The old red barn beside the Cruzes' farmhouse received a coat of fresh paint. D.C. had spent hours practicing his Tae Kwon Do kicks and punches with Randi, hoping to impress his black-belt dad.

"What happened?" Randi finally asked, dreading the answer.

D.C. kicked the wall of the shed.

"Hey," Pudge said softly. "Don't take it out on the hideout."

D.C. punched the door in response. "My dad isn't coming.

He told me he had to cancel the trip because he couldn't get out of work. "

Randi wrapped an arm around the boy and gave him a squeeze. "I know just how you feel. My dad just canceled our trip to New York because he has to work, too," she said.

"Yeah, but I bet *your* dad was telling the truth," D.C. replied. "He probably does have to work. Mine just has better things to do than hang out with me."

D.C. pulled a folded-up sheet of paper out of his *dobok* and passed it to Randi. It was an announcement for a martial arts tournament being held in Brooklyn over Thanksgiving weekend.

"I don't get it," Randi said. "What's this supposed to mean?"

"My dad lives in New Jersey. Brooklyn's less than an hour away. After he told me he'd canceled his trip, I put his name into Google. I found out he's going to be a judge at that tournament. He lied to get out of seeing me."

D.C. crossed his arms and bit his lower lip. Randi could tell he was trying not to cry.

"I'm really sorry, D.C.," said Pudge.

"Well," Randi told him, "at least we'll be stuck in Deer Creek together."

"And I never thought I'd hear myself say this, but I wish I could be stuck here, too," Pudge said.

The ninja detectives were busy feeling sorry for themselves when they heard the first ear-piercing scream.

"Puuuuuuuudddddggeee!"

A second voice joined in. "Help! Pudge! Help!" The cries seemed to be coming from right outside the shack.

The three ninjas were out the door in less than a second. In the orchard, there was nothing to see but trees, rotten apples, and dead leaves. Then a new round of screams directed their attention to the giant oak that stood a few feet from the hideout. A wooden platform had been built into the tree's upper reaches. D.C. called it his crow's nest. He'd built a rope and pulley system that he used as an elevator to reach the top. But the rope was lying in a useless pile on the ground. Even worse, high up in the branches, a little girl was dangling upside down, her right foot trapped in the narrow space between two branches. The girl's long pink coat had fallen over her head. She couldn't see anything—and all that the ninjas could see of her was her jeans and her arms, which were flailing wildly as she screamed in terror.

A second girl was crouched on a branch by the first girl's trapped foot. She seemed to have given up trying to help. Her eyes were squeezed shut as she shouted for her brother.

"Puuuuuuuudddddggeee!"

"I'm coming!" he shouted. "Hold tight, Laeleah."

Pudge handed D.C. his phone. "Call my dad and call the fire department."

"What on earth . . . ?" D.C.'s mom had heard the screams and come running outside in her nightgown. "Oh my Lord. Everyone stay put. I'll get the ladder!"

As she rushed back toward the barn, Pudge refused to wait. He threw the fallen rope over his shoulder and began scaling the tree. In her entire life, Randi had never seen anyone climb so quickly. He had reached the two girls in less than a minute. Randi watched as Pudge tied the rope into a lasso.

"Colonel Taylor and the fire department are on the way." D.C. had rushed back to Randi's side. "Is there anything we can do?"

Randi pointed to a blue plastic tarp that was covering up a hole in the hideout's roof. "Grab the tarp," Randi said. "We can hold it under the tree. We won't be able to catch her, but we might be able to break her fall a bit."

Up in the tree, Pudge had lowered the lasso he'd made. "Take the rope and put your arms through it," he told his upside-down sister.

D.C. returned with a blue tarp, which he and Randi stretched out beneath the dangling child.

"How? I can't see anything!" the girl shrieked.

"Take off your coat," Pudge said. "Let it drop to the ground."

The girl did as she was told. The coat hit the left side of the tarp and slid off. Randi shivered and adjusted her stance so the little girl would have a better chance of landing in the center of the tarp if she fell.

"Now take the rope. It's right in front of you," Pudge said, keeping his voice nice and calm. "You're going to be fine, Laeleah. As long as you do exactly what I tell you."

Laeleah grabbed at the rope circle.

"Now take the loop and make it tight around your chest." Pudge passed his end of the rope over a branch just above the spot where he was working. Slowly, he began to pull the girl upright. Laeleah was almost parallel to the ground when her foot suddenly slipped out of her shoe. Her twin sister shrieked and D.C. gasped. Randi held the tarp as tightly as she could. Above, the girl plunged toward the ground with a scream that made goose bumps erupt on Randi's skin. Then the rope around the child's chest jerked violently. Pudge's lasso had broken Laeleah's fall, and somehow he'd managed to keep the other end of the rope in his hands. His face ashen, he slowly lowered Laeleah to safety. Seconds later, D.C.'s mother arrived with the ladder, and Pudge helped his other sister Maya out of the tree.

"What were you doing up there?" Randi demanded when both Taylor girls were back on solid ground. Pudge seemed to be unable to speak. Saving his sisters had taken every last bit of his energy.

"We heard Pudge leave this morning," Maya confessed. "We followed him here."

"*Why?*" D.C. asked.

"They were trying to spy on him." Randi looked down at the two little imps. "Weren't you?"

Laeleah nodded guiltily.

They heard the sound of sirens coming toward the orchard.

Within seconds, a fire engine had appeared in the Crowleys' driveway. Pudge's father arrived less than two minutes later.

"Where are my girls?" he cried as he sprinted toward the oak tree. When he saw they were safe and sound, he dropped to his knees and wrapped his arms around them. "My princesses. I'm so glad you're okay. I was worried to death."

"And you!" There was rage in his eyes when Colonel Taylor turned on his son. "You, young man, are in serious trouble. How *dare* you bring these two girls here and let them climb a tree that big? If the fire department hadn't arrived in time—"

"Excuse me, Gordon?" D.C.'s mom interrupted. Pudge's dad spun around. His face was so terrifying that D.C.'s mom immediately took a step backward. "The fire department didn't save your daughter's life. Your son did. While I was trying to get the ladder out of the barn, he climbed all the way up to the top of that tree and rescued his little sister."

Pudge's father stood his ground. "Perhaps, but he should never have let them go up there in the first place."

"He didn't, sir," Randi stepped in to explain. "Maya and Laeleah followed Pudge here. We had no idea they were outside until we heard the screams. They climbed the tree so they could spy on us in our hideout."

"Is that true?" Colonel Taylor asked his daughters. They hesitated and then nodded their heads like a pair of bobblehead dolls. "Then get in the car. You two are under house arrest for the rest of the day. No, wait. Make that the rest of your *lives*."

As the girls ran to the car, Colonel Taylor addressed his son. "I'm very, very sorry, Kelly," he said. "I was wrong."

Pudge just looked at him for a moment. "I'm tired of being the responsible one," he said. "I quit."

"You quit?" Colonel Taylor responded.

"I think the boy's a bit shell-shocked, Gordon," D.C.'s mom said. "That's the first thing he's said since he came down from the tree."

Colonel Taylor put his arm around Pudge. "If you don't mind, I think I should take him home."

"See you at school tomorrow," Randi called out as Pudge and his dad walked away.

"I hope he's gonna be okay," D.C. whispered.

"He will," Randi said. "He's a ninja."

CHAPTER FOUR

THE SOFT SPOT

The homeroom bell had already rung by the time Randi shut her locker door. Her legs were gearing up for a sprint down the hall when she came to an unexpected halt. Five older girls were blocking her path. Amber-Grace Sutton stood in the center of the group, her hands on her hips and a snarl on her lips. Randi knew she could take Amber-Grace and her friends down with a single roundhouse kick. It didn't matter much that they were older and bigger than Randi was. But fighting would have gotten her in trouble at school, and her life stank enough already.

"What do you want?" Randi asked, keeping her voice steady and casual.

Amber-Grace flipped her long blond hair. Her glossy pink lips parted in a wide smile. Behind them was a set of perfect white teeth. "Revenge," she said. The other girls giggled.

"Yeah?" Randi shot back. "Well, I want my own private hovercraft, and my chances of getting what *I* want are a heck of a lot better than yours."

"That's what you think," Amber-Grace said. She took a step toward Randi. "You've got everyone in town saying I'm a thief. You're gonna pay for ruining my reputation."

Randi lifted her fists and assumed an attack pose. "Back off," she ordered the girl. "I don't want to hurt you."

"Go ahead," Amber-Grace challenged her. "Have you heard about our school's zero-tolerance policy when it comes to violence? You punch me, you're expelled for good."

"Not if I punch you outside of school," Randi was quick to point out.

"You really think Tae Kwon Do is going to save you?" Amber-Grace snickered. "I've lived in this town my entire life. I've gone to this school since kindergarten. I know all the best places to stage an ambush. My friends and I are going to snatch you one day when you least expect it. And once I've got you, Randi Rhodes, I'm gonna throw you in a closet where you'll never be found."

"Not that anyone would go looking for her anyway," one of the bullies said with a laugh.

"That's right," Amber-Grace said. "I almost forgot. Little Miss Tae Kwon Do hasn't got a mama, and her daddy must be awful busy. I haven't seen him around town in ages. You think that little old lady who lives at your house is gonna be able to protect you, Randi?"

Once again, she had hit Randi's soft spot. Randi felt her fists drop. "I don't need anyone to protect me," she told them. "I take care of myself." The last few words came out a bit wobbly. Randi could feel the tears in her eyes.

"There's only one way to do that, Randi. You're gonna have to leave Deer Creek."

"Yeah, why don't you go back to wherever you came from?" said another bully.

"We don't want you here," sneered another.

It actually seemed like a great idea. "Fine," Randi said. "Who wants to live in this dinky town anyway?" She spun on her heel and headed toward the school's front doors. She didn't care if it meant going to boarding school or getting herself sent to juvenile hall. Randi was going to leave Deer Creek and never come back.

"And just where do you think you're going, Miss Rhodes?" The vice principal poked her head out of the school's front office. "Do you have permission to leave?"

"No," Randi admitted. "But I couldn't stand to look at them anymore." She pointed down the hall to where the girls had been standing. But all five of them had vanished.

"Look at whom?" the vice principal asked.

"They were just . . ."

"Get to class, Miss Rhodes," the vice principal said with a huff. "You can tell me all about the school's ghosts at detention this afternoon."

Three hours later, Randi was in the lunchroom, which was packed with students in grades five through eight. Randi could feel Amber-Grace and her friends watching her as she filled a tray with soggy gray meatloaf and yellow mashed potatoes.

D.C. took a peek over his shoulder. "You want me to go over there and make them mind their own business?" he asked.

"And then what?" Randi asked with a sigh. "Are you going to do it again tomorrow? And the day after that and the day after that? Those girls are just going to keep on tormenting me until I lose my mind or get myself kicked out of school." Randi had to admit it was a brilliant strategy. She couldn't believe Amber-Grace had been the one who'd come up with it.

Randi and D.C. carried their trays to a table across the cafeteria. Randi picked up her fork, but the stench that was rising from the food on her plate made her nauseous. Then the smell of meat loaf was overwhelmed by the sickly sweet fragrance of a dozen different kinds of flowers. Amber-Grace and her friends were parading by, smelling like they'd just bathed in perfume. They slowed down as they passed Randi and D.C.'s table.

"So my *mom* promised we could go for mani-pedis this afternoon," Amber-Grace announced, speaking loudly enough for everyone in the cafeteria to hear.

"That's awesome. Isn't it great having a *mom*?" one of the other girls asked. It sounded like she was reading the words off a piece of paper. Amber-Grace's friends had clearly been coached.

"I really love to go shopping with my *mom*," a third girl said. "Don't you?"

"You know what happens to girls without *moms*?" asked a fourth. "They start to turn into boys."

"You mean like Randi Rhodes?" Amber-Grace asked.

"Yeah," said one of the others. "I mean look at her. It's supersad, isn't it? I think my baby brother has the same exact outfit she's wearing."

"That's enough!" D.C. stood up from the table. "You guys get out of here before I go find a teacher."

The girls giggled. "Before you get a *teacher*? I guess it *is* true what they say about boys who grow up without their dads," Amber-Grace added.

"What's that?" one of her friends asked.

"They're *sissies*," Amber-Grace whispered conspiratorially.

Randi had to grab D.C. to stop him from hurling himself across the table at the girl.

A bell rang. It was time for the seventh and eighth graders to return to their classes. "Gotta go. We'll see you two again soon," Amber-Grace sang.

"It's going to take an awful lot of self-control to keep from punching her," D.C. said.

"Self-control is overrated," Randi grumbled. "Hey, look who's here."

Pudge was standing in the center of the cafeteria, searching for his friends. It wasn't the same Pudge they'd said good-bye to the day before. This Pudge was bouncing on his heels and beaming from ear to ear.

"He's looking a million times happier than he did yester-day," D.C. said.

"I haven't seen him smile like that in ages," Randi said. "Maybe his dad let him choose Maya and Laeleah's punish-ment."

Randi held up an arm. Pudge spotted it and hurried over. The wide smile on his face turned into a quizzical look the closer he got.

"What's wrong with you guys?" he asked. "You look like you just lost your best friend. And I know that's not possible 'cause here I am!" The smile was back.

"You're certainly in a good mood," Randi mumbled.

"He wasn't at the bank, remember?" D.C. explained. "Amber-Grace and her crew aren't out to get *him*."

"I have no idea what you're talking about," Pudge said, and he didn't seem particularly interested in finding out. "But I do have some news that may just brighten your miserable lives."

"I doubt it," Randi said.

"Oh yeah? Well, how about this? My sisters got grounded for following me to the hideout yesterday morning. And I got a reward for saving Grace's life. Mom's driving the girls up to Boston tomorrow. My dad and I are going by ourselves Tuesday. No girls. No giggling. No watching *The Little Mermaid* three times in a row."

"That's great, Pudge," Randi said weakly. "I'm happy for you."

"You don't get it, do you?" Pudge's grin was so wide that it looked like it might split his head in half. "What are we gonna pass on the way up to Boston?"

"The Cumberland Gap?" D.C. asked.

"What?" Pudge shot the boy a look. "We're going to pass *New York City*. Know anybody who might need a ride?"

Randi nearly leaped out of her seat with joy. "Are you kidding? You can drive me? Have you asked your dad? Is it okay with him?"

Pudge sat back. "No, I'm not kidding. Yes, we can drive you to Brooklyn. And no, I didn't ask my dad. He was the one who suggested it. He also wondered if D.C. might want to come along for the ride."

"Me?" D.C. gasped.

"Yep. He said you're welcome to come with us to Boston if you want."

"Actually," Randi said mischievously. "I think I might have a better idea."

"How could anything get any better?" D.C. marveled.

"I dunno. How would you both like to hang out in Brooklyn with me? My aunt has a huge apartment and she's supercool. I'm sure she wouldn't mind a few extra guests."

"*I* mind," Herb Rhodes said, putting his foot down. "Gigi isn't used to kids. Heck, Gigi acts like a kid herself. I don't think it's a good idea for the three of you to impose on her."

Randi's heart was sinking fast. "But, Dad, I texted Gigi this afternoon. She told me she'd love to have the company. She says she'll be lonely without guests on Thanksgiving."

"Gigi doesn't know what it's like having three kids around," Herb responded.

"We'll be on our best behavior!" Randi pleaded.

"Says the girl who spent two hours in detention after school today. Thought I didn't know about that, didn't ya?" He tapped his temple with an index finger as he slurped up a forkful of noodles.

"Why are you doing this?" Randi asked. She genuinely didn't understand. "Why are you treating me like a little kid again? I thought I proved to you that I could take care of myself. I mean, come on! You just wrote a book about me and my friends!"

Herb shook his head and swallowed. "I wrote a book about three kids playing detective in Deer Creek, Tennessee. You're talking about going to Brooklyn, Randi. That's a whole other story."

Across the table from Randi, Mei-Ling cleared her throat. She rarely interfered in the Rhodeses' arguments. But this time she seemed to have something to say.

"Go ahead and tell Randi she's crazy, Mei-Ling," Herb said.

"Who is Gigi?" Mei-Ling asked instead. Randi stared at her. Then she looked over at her father, who was staring at Mei-Ling, too. The old woman must have heard Gigi's name a thousand times.

"Gigi is my wife's sister," Herb replied.

"Oh," Mei-Ling said. "Were they close?"

"Very," Herb said. He'd stopped shoveling food into his mouth. "Gigi knew my wife better than anyone. They were as close as two people can get."

"She must miss Olivia-Kay very much," Mei-Ling said. "Gigi doesn't have any family left in Brooklyn, does she?"

"No," Herb said. "Her parents passed away a long time ago. That's why she has so much room to spare. She inherited their enormous old apartment."

Mei-Ling nodded. "Then maybe Gigi didn't invite Randi to be nice. Maybe she needs to spend time with the girl her sister left behind. And maybe Randi needs to see the woman who knew her mom better than anyone."

Randi sat back in awe. It was a master move. Mei-Ling had made her point—and left no room for argument. And she'd done it without raising her voice or getting riled up. Randi glanced over at her dad. He was staring into the distance, looking at nothing in particular. It was the same look he'd often worn after Randi's mom had died.

"Dad?" she asked.

The life came back to his eyes. "Mei-Ling is right," he announced. "Maybe it would be a good idea for you and Gigi to spend some time together. Let me just talk to Colonel Taylor and find out if he knows what he's gotten himself into."

"Yay!" Randi hopped out of her chair and rushed around

the table to give them both hugs. "Thank you," she told Mei-Ling.

"Just promise me you'll come back," Mei-Ling whispered in her ear.

CHAPTER FIVE

THE LADY IN BLACK

Colonel Taylor ran a tight ship. Before they climbed into the silver SUV, each of the kids was handed a typewritten list of rules.

- No eating in the car.
- No littering.
- No shouting or loud talking.
- No shoes on the seats.
- Earphones must be used at all times.
- Food stops and bathroom breaks at 06:00, 09:00, 12:00, 15:00, and 18:00. Plan your fluid intake accordingly.

"Sorry," Pudge mumbled, looking horribly embarrassed. "My dad thinks he's still in the army."

"And here I was worrying that you guys might give the colonel trouble." Herb Rhodes laughed. "I'm going to borrow that list for *our* next trip."

"*I'd* be fine," Randi said. "You're the one who wouldn't make it as far as Virginia."

"You're probably right," Herb Rhodes admitted. "I break all of those rules just driving to the grocery store." He slid Randi's suitcase into the SUV's trunk. "You going to be okay?" he asked quietly.

"Yep," Randi replied. Up until that second, she'd been eager to leave. But now she realized that she hadn't spent a single night away from her dad since her mom died. She wasn't sure she was ready. "You?"

"I think so," Herb told her. "I'll miss you like crazy, though."

"I'll miss you, too." The hug Randi gave him lasted long enough for everyone else to get in the car and Colonel Taylor to start the engine.

"You better go," Herb Rhodes told his daughter. "But please come back soon."

It was just a joke, but it reminded Randi of what Mei-Ling had said at dinner. *Just promise me you'll come back.* Deep down, everyone seemed to think she might stay in Brooklyn. The possibility had never occurred to her. But now that the thought was in her head, Randi knew it wasn't just going to go away.

Within hours, Randi had gained a newfound appreciation for her father—and had started to feel a bit sorry for Pudge. Life with Colonel Taylor was not easy. The kids were allowed to purchase only the healthiest items whenever they stopped for food. Randi tried her best to convince Pudge's dad that French fries were essential road trip nutrition, but she couldn't get him to budge on the matter. Bathroom breaks were timed with the stopwatch function on Colonel Taylor's cell phone, and taking more than three minutes was deemed unacceptable. Inside the car, the kids were forced to speak in whispers.

Thankfully, Mei-Ling had stocked up on New York City travel guides. Randi had almost asked her to take them back to the store. After all, she had lived in Brooklyn almost her entire life. But as it turned out, the guides were proving quite useful.

"Where in Brooklyn do the gangsters live?" D.C. asked. He had a map of the five New York City boroughs open in front of him. "Can we go there?"

"The gangsters?" Randi tried not to laugh.

"You know," D.C. said. "Wise guys. Made men. Mafia types."

"You watch *way* too much television," Pudge told him.

"I don't think we want to hang out with gangsters. And I'm pretty sure they don't want to hang out with us," Randi said. "But my aunt lives right across from the Brooklyn Museum. They've got an amazing collection of Egyptian mummies. And there's usually some sort of cool exhibit. Let's see what they've got going on while we're in town." She used her smartphone to call up the Brooklyn Museum's website. "Oh," she said with disappointment. "Looks like it's an exhibit of Fabergé eggs."

"What's a Fabergé?" D.C. asked. "And what's so great about its eggs?"

It might have been the first time that Randi had ever heard Colonel Taylor laugh. "Fabergé was a man, not an animal," he informed D.C. from the driver's seat. "He made beautiful jeweled Easter eggs for the last Russian tsar and his family. Most of them are priceless."

"Sounds awesome," Randi droned. The last thing in the world that she wanted to see was a bunch of fancy-schmancy Easter eggs. "I think I'd rather spend time with the mummies."

"I don't usually go for the froufrou stuff myself," said Colonel Taylor. "But I had an interesting experience at a Fabergé exhibit once. Since then, they've always felt a bit magical and mysterious to me."

Randi knew the start of a good story when she heard one. The three kids in the backseat put down their phones and magazines.

"What happened?" Pudge asked his dad.

"Well, it was before any of you kids were born. I was a security expert for the US Army, and I was sent to New York on an assignment. The Russian government was lending some Fabergé Imperial Eggs to a museum there called the Frick."

"I know that place," Randi said. "The museum is in a beautiful old mansion. My mom used to take me there sometimes when my dad was out of town." Randi remembered skipping across the lush carpets and around the centuries-old furniture as she and her mom had passed from one stunningly beautiful room to the next. Randi had loved the museum's little bronze gods and goddesses best, while her mother had spent most of their visits admiring the Frick's priceless paintings in their gilded frames. Olivia-Kay Rhodes had been an artist herself, and she'd never seemed more content than when she was surrounded by art.

"The building wasn't always a museum," Colonel Taylor confirmed. "It was originally a wealthy man's home. That's one reason the Russians were so keen to have the electronic security systems inspected. The eggs are the perfect things to steal. They're small, so they are easy to transport and hide. And each one of them is worth millions."

"Were there weaknesses in the security system?" Randi asked.

"None that I could find at first," Colonel Taylor admitted. "Which is why I was so surprised by what happened."

"There was a robbery?" D.C. asked.

"No," Pudge's dad responded. "But there was a break-in the evening after the Fabergé exhibit opened. The crowds had been incredible all day, but by eight o'clock, I finally had the building almost completely to myself. The only other people who were supposed to be in the museum were three security guards who were constantly making their rounds. I had already finished my assignment, and it was my last night on the job. All of the museum's doors were locked and the alarms were activated. I'd learned how to avoid tripping them, but it wasn't an easy feat. You had to know where to step—and what not to touch.

"The room where the Fabergé eggs were displayed was quite eerie at night. There were two dozen glass displays, each with a single egg inside. The room itself was dark, but the glass boxes were lit up. It made it very easy to see the eggs—and very difficult to see anything else. So that night, when I entered the room, I didn't spot her at first, and I'm certain she didn't see me either."

"Who was it?" Pudge asked.

"A burglar?" Randi asked.

"A ghost?" D.C. asked.

"It was a young woman," said Colonel Taylor. "She was wearing a black trench coat and a short black wig. And she was sketching one of the eggs on a pad of paper."

"What did you do?" Randi asked.

"Well, I approached her, of course. She smiled and kept on drawing. I asked her what she thought she was doing, and she told me to wait a moment while she finished her sketch."

"And you let her?" Pudge sounded shocked.

Colonel Taylor shrugged. "She seemed like a nice young lady. And her art was exceptional. I thought it deserved to be finished. When she put down her pencil, she kindly answered my question. She said she was doing research for a book. The egg she was drawing was going to play an important role. She claimed she'd tried to visit the museum during the day, but the exhibit had been too crowded to do any sketching."

"She said *that* was the reason she'd broken into a museum

at night?" D.C. asked. "To do some *sketching*? And you believed her?"

"I was a bit skeptical at first," Pudge's dad admitted. "But then I asked how she'd managed to get in without setting off any alarms, and she was more than happy to tell me. *You don't know about the secret dumbwaiters, do you?* she said. Turns out, she had examined the original building plans and had found the perfect place to hide until the museum closed. The dumbwaiters were little elevators that the servants used in the old days to transport necessary items from one floor to the next."

"Wow," Randi said. "And she figured out where they were? I'm starting to like this lady."

"I guess you could say she saved my behind," Colonel Taylor said. "If a real crook had found that hole in the security system, it could have caused a whole heap of trouble."

"That's such a great story," D.C. said. "Kinda makes me want to have a look at those Easter egg thingies."

"And I haven't even gotten to the best part yet," said the colonel. "I let the woman go, of course, but I did take down her name and phone number. Guess what name she gave me?"

The kids waited breathlessly for the answer.

"She said her name was Glenn Street."

Randi laughed. "That's hilarious!"

"It's not that funny if you think about it. I'd never heard the name before. Remember when this all happened, Randi. When did the first Glenn Street novel come out?"

Randi felt like she'd been walloped. "It came out when I was one year old," she whispered. "My dad started writing the book after I was born."

"Whoa!" Pudge said. "I think my mind just got blown!"

"Wait." D.C.'s brow was furrowed. "Does that mean that the woman's name really *was* Glenn Street?"

"To this day, I haven't figured it out," Colonel Taylor said. "A few years after the incident at the museum, I walked into a bookstore and saw a novel with the name Glenn Street on the cover. I was convinced it was the book the woman had been writing—until I opened the jacket flap and saw Herb Rhodes's face. I even bought it, thinking the woman might have used a pen name. There wasn't a single mention of Fabergé eggs in the entire novel. But that, Miss Rhodes, is how I became such a big fan of your father's work."

"Maybe my dad knows who it was," Randi said.

"That was one of the first things I asked him when he and I met in Deer Creek."

"And?" Randi asked.

"And Herb said he had no idea. He didn't seem to want to talk about Glenn Street, and I didn't want to pry."

"Really?" Randi had never known her father to turn down an opportunity to discuss Glenn Street. He might have stopped writing about her, but she was still one of the great loves of his life.

Then a bolt of inspiration struck. Randi pulled her wallet

out of her backpack. Tucked into one of the pockets was a picture she took with her wherever she went.

"Sir?" she asked. "Does this look like the woman you saw in the museum?"

Colonel Taylor took a quick glance at the photo Randi had placed in his hand. Within seconds, he had pulled to the side of the road. Once the car had stopped, he took out his reading glasses and had a closer look at the picture.

"That's her!" he exclaimed. "She has different hair in this picture, but I'm almost positive that's the mysterious woman at the Frick!"

"That's my mom," Randi told him.

The photo she had handed Colonel Taylor showed Olivia-Kay Rhodes sitting on a stoop in Brooklyn, proudly holding a two-week-old Randi. ☠

☠ Go to Appendix B to complete the Ninja Task!

CHAPTER SIX

GIGI

It was six o'clock when the Taylor family SUV rolled to a stop in front of the colossal apartment building where Randi's aunt Gigi lived. The three kids hadn't spoken a word for half an hour. That's when they had spotted the Statue of Liberty standing in the New York harbor with a blazing torch in her hand. Behind the statue were the magnificent skyscrapers of Manhattan's financial district. D.C. had whistled appreciatively. He'd never seen anything like it. Randi had, but the beauty of it still had the power to render her speechless. She was finally home, she thought, and she wiped away a tear before anyone could see.

Now the daylight was slipping away. Across the street from Gigi's building, the Brooklyn Museum was lit up like a lantern. It resembled an ancient Greek temple, complete with columns and statues and a giant dome on top. But a modern glass addition on the ground floor now served as an entrance. Long cloth banners were hanging above, swaying and fluttering in the strong autumn winds. Each banner featured a different brightly colored bejeweled egg. Together, the banners read, FABERGÉ: SECRETS OF THE TSAR.

"What does that mean?" Randi asked Colonel Taylor. Now that there might have been a connection between Fabergé and her mom, she couldn't get enough of the subject.

"*Tsar* is the Russian word for king," he explained. "The rule of the last tsar ended in 1917. He and his family were executed when the Communists took power."

"And what about the 'secrets' part?" Randi inquired. "What do the tsar's secrets have to do with Easter eggs?"

"They weren't just Easter eggs," Colonel Taylor said. "Fabergé made fifty Imperial Eggs. Each and every one of them had a treasure hidden inside."

"What kind of treasures?" Pudge asked.

"I remember one opened up to reveal a tiny palace carved in gold. It was a perfect replica of one of the tsar's palaces. Other eggs had miniature paintings or figurines."

Randi could smell a mystery. "Do you remember which egg my mom . . . I mean the lady in black . . . was sketching when you saw her at the Frick?"

"I don't," Colonel Taylor admitted. "But maybe if you visit the museum you can try to guess which one caught her eye. Looks like the Fabergé exhibit opens this Sunday."

"Can I go too?" Pudge begged.

"No," Colonel Taylor said, his voice getting gruff again. "We'll be in Boston with your grandmother. We won't have time for fun." He stopped, as if he'd found his own words strange. "What I meant to say is that we're on a tight schedule. We don't have room to add anything else to the itinerary. Now, everyone out of the car. Let's get this luggage upstairs."

"It's true. We never have time for fun," Pudge grumbled once his father was out of the car.

"Rannnddddeeeeee!" Gigi threw open the door, grabbed her niece, and spun her around the room. "I've missed you sooooooo much!"

She set Randi down and had a good look at her. Randi stumbled a step backward, dizzy from the spinning. "Oh my goodness. You're all grown up and dangerous!" Gigi proclaimed. "Please tell me you're still fighting crime and kicking bad-guy butt!"

Randi laughed. Gigi always knew what she wanted to hear. The spunky blonde was a younger, fairer version of her sister, Olivia-Kay. There had been almost eight years between them. Randi's mom had practically raised Gigi, and Randi had always felt that Gigi was more like a sister than an aunt. Unfortunately, they'd never had a chance to spend much time together. Gigi had been away at school for most of Randi's childhood. She'd returned to Brooklyn when Randi's mother had died—and left to work overseas a few months later.

"Gigi, I'd like you to meet my friends D.C. and Pudge," Randi said. "And this is Pudge's dad, Colonel Taylor."

D.C. held out a hand, but he got a hug. Much to their surprise, Pudge and his dad got hugs, too.

"You have a lovely apartment," Colonel Taylor said, admiring the spacious living room with its stunning view of the museum across the street. "And quite large by New York standards."

"It belonged to my parents," Gigi explained. "My sister and I grew up here, and I moved back in after I got out of school. It's way too big for me, but I couldn't bear to give it up. And I love having guests. I'm so thrilled that you could join me for Thanksgiving," she said, putting to rest any suggestion that Gigi might feel inconvenienced. "I was heartbroken when I thought you might not be coming."

"Ms. Daly, I think there's been a—" Colonel Taylor started to say.

"Come on. Come on! We'll catch up later." She was grabbing her coat. "The museum closes at eight tonight. We just have enough time to say hello to the mummies. Then we're going to hop in a cab and head to this *amazing* Ethiopian restaurant I know."

Colonel Taylor didn't budge. "It was a pleasure to meet you, Ms. Daly," he said. "But I'm afraid my son and I must get going. We're trying to reach Boston tonight, and we have five hours left on the road."

But Gigi wouldn't take no for an answer. "Then we'll skip the mummies and head straight to dinner. You'd have to stop to eat anyway, wouldn't you?"

Gigi didn't know that Colonel Taylor budgeted exactly fifteen minutes for meal consumption during road trips. Randi still had indigestion from gulping down a salami sandwich at lunch.

"Please, Dad?" Pudge begged.

Randi expected to hear Colonel Taylor say no. But he looked down at his son's face and, for once, the army man surprised her. "I do have a soft spot for Ethiopian food," he admitted. "All right, then. *Dinner*. But after that, Pudge, we're back on the road."

"Thank you, Dad!" Pudge did his signature victory dance, which made him look like a robot with a few gears missing.

"You're welcome, Pudge." His father sighed and rolled his eyes. There was nothing he despised more than the victory dance.

"Wow, that was amazing!" Gigi exclaimed. "You've got some serious moves, kid. Will you teach me some of them later?"

"Sure!" Pudge cried.

From the outside, the Ethiopian restaurant looked like a regular storefront on a rather dingy avenue in the heart of Brooklyn. But as soon as the kids set foot inside, it was clear they had entered another land. Mouthwatering fragrances wafted through the air. Diners sat around circular tables, sharing food from a single giant platter set in the middle. Each platter held a number of brightly colored dishes that Randi had never encountered. There were no plates and no utensils—just a stack of purplish, spongy pancakes that the diners were using to scoop up their food.

"Everyone here is eating with their hands!" D.C. whispered.

Gigi giggled. "That's what you're supposed to do at an Ethiopian restaurant," she explained. "That soft, flat bread they give you is called *injera*. You use it instead of a fork."

When they were taken to their table, Gigi and Colonel Taylor were seated side by side.

"What sort of work do you do?" Randi heard Colonel Taylor try to make small talk with Gigi. She smiled. She could tell the colonel was expecting to hear that Gigi was busy living off the fat of the land.

"Me?" Gigi answered in her childlike voice. "I'm a doctor."

If he'd been sipping water at that moment, the colonel would have done a spit take. "You're a *doctor*?" he sputtered. "What kind of doctor?"

"I'm a neurosurgeon," Gigi replied.

"You cut open people's heads and operate on their brains?" D.C. asked. "Cool."

"Thanks! I think so," Gigi said. "I just got back from a year-long tour in Cambodia with Doctors Without Borders. I need a little rest, so I'm taking a few months off to write a book."

"Fiction?" Colonel Taylor seemed to be too shocked to utter more than one word.

"Nope," Gigi said. "It's about the latest advances in clinical electromyography. I know it sounds like a snooze, but for neurologists, it's practically a thriller."

"Very impressive," Colonel Taylor said. "I would have assumed you were an artist of some sort."

"Oh, I am!" Gigi replied. "I'm working on a ceramics project now. I'm doing a modern take on canopic jars—you know the vessels the Egyptians used to store organs after they were removed from mummies during the embalming process. That's one of the reasons I loved growing up across from the museum. It's an endless source of inspiration. You know, it's too bad that Pudge won't have a chance to see the mummies. . . ."

She continued to talk, but Randi was stuck on two little words. *The museum.* It took Randi back to the story she'd heard on the drive to New York.

"Excuse me," she told the group. "I'm just going to step outside and call my dad. He'll want to know that we got here okay."

"Are you sure going outside is a good idea?" Colonel Taylor asked. "It's getting pretty dark out there, and this isn't Deer Creek."

"Just stay close to the entrance," Gigi said. "And if anyone bugs you, you have my permission to give him a good solid roundhouse kick in the rump."

Outside, a cold wind was blowing down the avenue. Randi turned the collar of her jacket up, pulled out her phone, and dialed her dad's number.

He answered immediately. "Randi! I just had my phone out to call you!"

"Great minds think alike," Randi said. "Where are you?"

"In a cab to my hotel in rainy Seattle," said Herb Rhodes. "Where it happens to be a beautiful sunny day. How 'bout you?"

"We're at Gigi's favorite Ethiopian restaurant on Fourth Avenue."

Herb groaned with jealousy. "I love that place. How was the ride?"

"Interesting. Pudge's dad is really strict. But I did hear a good story." Randi started off cautiously. She was suddenly feeling a bit nervous.

"I'm all ears," said her dad.

"We were talking about a new Fabergé egg exhibit that's coming to the Brooklyn Museum, and Colonel Taylor said he once caught a woman who'd snuck past security at a similar exhibit at the Frick museum. The lady told him her name was Glenn Street. Two years before you started writing the Glenn Street books."

Herb Rhodes cleared his throat, the way he did whenever he was feeling uncomfortable. Randi knew in an instant she was onto something. "Yes, he told me the same story. It has to be a coincidence."

"I don't think it was a coincidence, Dad. I showed him a picture of Mom. He ID'd her as the lady at the Frick."

The statement met with utter silence on the other end of the line.

"Dad?" Randi asked.

He cleared his throat once more. "Yes?"

"Do you think it was Mom? You guys were living in the city back then and you'd been married for a year."

"I don't know," Herb Rhodes said. "I suppose anything is possible. Listen, Randi, my cab just got to the hotel. I need to check in and get ready for an event tonight. Can I call you in the morning?"

"Sure," Randi said. She couldn't figure out what had just happened. For some reason, her dad sounded determined to get off the phone. She knew she'd just uncovered a mystery, and she couldn't wait to find out what Gigi knew.

"Thanks. And, Randi, I know Gigi has had a hard time getting over your mom's death. Don't go asking a lot of questions that will make her go through it again."

"Okay, Dad," Randi said. Great minds really did think alike.

"Good night, sweetheart," he said. And the line went dead.

Randi was stunned. As she made her way back into the restaurant, it felt as if her body was moving on its own. When D.C. saw her approaching the table, which was now filled with food, he jumped up to greet her.

"Guess what? Guess what?" he asked twice with excitement.

"What?" Randi replied robotically.

"Pudge's dad says he can stay! Gigi talked him into it. Didn't she, Pudge?"

Pudge looked like he'd just gotten the shock of his life. "Yeah," he confirmed, his face breaking into a wide smile. "I don't know how she did it, but yeah!"

Randi glanced over at the two adults who were seated side by side. Gigi, in her victory, seemed absolutely thrilled. Colonel Taylor wore a more complex expression. He looked to Randi like a man who was on the verge of conducting a dangerous experiment.

CHAPTER SEVEN

THE WATCHER

Someone was shaking Randi awake. When she opened her eyes, she could see that the sun had just started to rise.

"What time is it?" she mumbled. Pudge, reveling in his newfound freedom, had tried his best to keep his friends up all night. D.C. had passed out sometime around eleven. Randi hadn't lasted much longer.

"It's seven a.m." Gigi was whispering in Randi's ear. "Put on a couple layers of warm clothes that you can move in. Then meet me in the living room."

Randi was groggy when she emerged from the bedroom. "This warm enough?" she asked. She was wearing sweatpants over a pair of jeans—and two hoodies on top of each other.

"Perfect," said Gigi. "Let's go."

It was the day before Thanksgiving, and the city was quiet. Randi followed her aunt across Eastern Parkway, past a single car that was stopped at the streetlight. On the other side of the avenue, a high gate blocked the entrance to the Brooklyn Botanic Garden. A wrought-iron fence circled the rest of the park. Gigi stepped off the sidewalk and followed the fence as it scaled a small hill. Halfway up, she hopped on top of a boulder that sat next to iron bars, and then she reached up and grabbed a tree branch above her head. From there, she pulled herself up until she could put one sneaker on top of the fence. Then she dropped silently to the other side.

Randi matched her aunt's every move, and soon they were both inside the deserted botanical garden.

"For the record, I'm a lifetime member of the Brooklyn Botanic Garden," Gigi stated. "I just prefer to use my own entrance."

"How did you figure out how to get in like that?" Randi whispered as they set off across the grass.

"Your mom taught me," Gigi said.

"*My mom* knew how to break into the Brooklyn Botanic Garden?"

"Sure. We lived across the street, remember? She and I used to come here when we were kids. Want to see our favorite spot?"

"Yeah!" Randi said.

"Good, 'cause we're almost there."

They'd come to a small Japanese-style building that sat beside an emerald-green lake. Across from it, rising out of the water, was a large wooden structure painted a bright reddish orange. It looked like a gate to another world.

"It's called a torii," Gigi said. "The Japanese believe that torii are gateways to sacred spaces."

"It does feel sacred here," Randi whispered. A cold morning breeze rustled the garden's remaining leaves and set the trees swaying. There was no sound of traffic—nothing to remind you that you were in the middle of New York City.

"Your mom and I always thought so, too. This way," Gigi said, leading her to a path that wound around the lake. Giant koi swam over to greet them. They glittered orange, gold, blue, and silver beneath the surface of the water.

"Wow. It's almost like they recognize you," Randi said.

"I'm sure they do. Koi are highly intelligent creatures, and I've known some of them since I was your age."

"Whoa. Those fish were around in the 1990s?"

"Yep. Quite a few of them are even older than I am. Koi can live to be fifty years old." Gigi reached into her jacket pocket and pulled out a handful of brown nuggets. She gave half to Randi and tossed the rest into the lake. "Fish food. You're not really supposed to feed the little buggers," she admitted. "But to me they're not fish. They're more like old friends."

After a short walk around the water, Randi and Gigi arrived at the waterfall that fed the lake. A stream of clear water cascaded over two sets of rocks, surrounded by trees and bushes. It had to be the most beautiful spot in Brooklyn.

Gigi took a seat on a rock beside the waterfall and motioned for Randi to sit beside her. Then she pulled a thermos and two paper cups out of her knapsack. The air filled with the fragrance of cocoa as she poured a stream of steaming liquid into the cups. Randi took a sip. It was as rich and delicious as a chocolate bar.

Randi had so many questions she wanted to ask. But she couldn't get her father's warning out of her head. There might be things her aunt didn't want to discuss. Olivia-Kay Rhodes's death had been hard on everyone.

Gigi was the one who finally broke the silence. "You know, you remind me so much of your mother."

"Everyone says that," Randi said. "It's because we have the same crazy red hair."

"Your hair is red?" Gigi joked, flicking one of Randi's ringlets with her finger. Then her smile turned sad. "No, it's not just the hair. You have the same spirit."

It was nice of her to say, but Randi just didn't buy it. She couldn't quite believe that she shared the same spirit as her sweet, artistic mother. "What was she like when you guys were kids?" Randi asked.

Gigi smiled. "Olivia-Kay was what people used to call a tomboy, which is an old-fashioned word for a girl who likes to climb trees and go on adventures."

"Don't a lot of girls like to do stuff like that?" Randi asked.

"Exactly," Gigi said. "But I have to admit, your mom was more daring than most girls—or boys for that matter."

"She was?" Randi asked.

Gigi's smile widened, as if she was recalling a whole lifetime of fond memories. "Oh yes," she said. "Olivia-Kay was always convincing me to do the craziest things. It's amazing either of us survived to see adulthood."

It felt like Gigi was talking about someone Randi had never met. "What sort of stuff did she convince you to do?"

"Well, once she had us hide in the Museum of Natural History until it closed. She wanted see what it was like to have the place to ourselves."

"That sounds awfully familiar," Randi said, remembering Colonel Taylor's story about the Frick museum. "I bet it was a lot of fun."

"It was—while it lasted. But the only thing we had to eat was a package of Pop Rocks, and a guard passing by heard us having our dinner." Gigi laughed. "Then another time, she convinced me to spend two weeks spying on one of our neighbors downstairs. My sister was convinced that the woman was on the run from the law. And you know what? It turned out Olivia-Kay was right! The lady had embezzled almost a million dollars from some business in Detroit. We both got a reward for calling the cops."

Randi frowned. Gigi had to be pulling her leg. "You're making this stuff up, aren't you?"

"Absolutely not," Gigi said. "Just ask your dad."

"But Mom wasn't like that when I knew her!" Randi argued.

"We had a lot of fun, but I always thought she was the sort of person who liked to play it safe."

"Oh yeah?" Gigi asked. "Wasn't your mom the one who convinced you to take Tae Kwon Do? And didn't she take you to all the cool hidden spots in Prospect Park? And I distinctly remember the day she dared you to eat barbequed crickets. Think about it, Randi. Wasn't she the one who taught you how to be the awesome kid that you are?"

Randi realized just how much she had taken for granted. She'd always known she had the best mother in the world. But she'd never even suspected how fabulous Olivia-Kay Rhodes had really been.

"I wish I'd figured it out a bit earlier," Randi said softly.

"You were young when she died. You're figuring it out now," Gigi said. Then she paused. "You know, Olivia-Kay and I came here together once when she was sick. She asked me to look after you. Not in a *make sure Randi eats well and gets good grades* sort of way. She wanted you to have the kind of childhood we had. An adventure every week, she told me. I swore I would do whatever I could. But then you moved away." She paused and her face grew dark. "I was very angry when your father called me in Cambodia and told me he was going to take you down South. It meant I couldn't keep my promise to my sister when I got back home."

"If it's any consolation, I was pretty mad, too," Randi said.

Gigi nodded. "I bet. What's it like down there, anyway?

Things still as exciting as they were last summer?"

"Hardly," Randi scoffed. "I'm starting to think I might die of boredom before I turn thirteen."

"Not if I have anything to do with it," Gigi said. "I have big plans for this weekend. I was talking to your friend D.C. He told me there's a martial arts tournament in town. Isn't that right up your alley?"

"Yeah!" Randi said. Why hadn't she thought of it?

"And how 'bout we forget having turkey on Thanksgiving and go somewhere amazing instead?"

"Yeah!" Randi cried. It was going to be the best weekend ever.

"And, Randi?" Suddenly Gigi wasn't kidding around anymore. "If you ever want to come back to Brooklyn, I have a bedroom with your name on it."

"Really?" Randi asked.

"Yes," Gigi told her. "Anytime." Then she drained the last of her cocoa, stood up, and offered Randi a hand. "Now, let's get home. It's time to introduce your friends to the wonders of New York City bagels."

They stepped through the front door to hear a yelp come from one of the bedrooms. They hurried to investigate. Pudge was sitting upright in his bed, staring at the clock on his cell phone.

"It's nine fifteen!"

"And?" Gigi asked.

"Why did you let me sleep so late?"

"Because you were *tired*," Randi said.

Pudge couldn't seem to think of a response. "My dad wakes us up at six thirty sharp," he explained. "I've never been asleep at nine fifteen before."

"Well, you should try sleeping till ten," Gigi told him. "I swear, it's even better."

"Hey!" D.C. called out from behind them, his voice a loud whisper. Randi turned to see him already dressed, a pair of binoculars hanging around his neck. "Come here! Come here! You're not going to believe this!"

"Why are you whispering?" Randi asked.

"You'll see," D.C. said.

"This better be good," Pudge grumbled, slipping out of bed. "I was about to find out what it feels like to sleep until ten a.m."

D.C. led them back to his room and headed for the window where the venetian blinds were still down. He pulled them apart a few inches. "Look down there!" he ordered.

Randi peeked through the blinds. Aside from a lady with a green Mohawk who was walking six pit bulls at once, there wasn't anything to see. "This isn't Tennessee," Randi told D.C. "We have stores that sell things besides camouflage and baseball hats. You're gonna see people wearing all kinds of crazy stuff while you're here. Might as well get used to it."

"What?" D.C.'s forehead wrinkled with confusion. He pushed Randi aside and had another look at the street. "I

guess he's gone," he muttered to himself. Then he yanked up the blinds and let the light into the room. "You thought I was talking about that woman with the dogs? My mom's got a million tattoos. You think I'm impressed by a Mohawk? And just for the record, there are a lot of people in Tennessee who don't wear camo *or* baseball hats. I know you two Yankees don't understand—"

"Okay, okay," Pudge interrupted, rubbing his eyes as they adjusted to the bright sunlight. "If you weren't talking about the Mohawk, then what *were* you talking about?"

"Randi and Gigi woke me up when they left this morning. I got out of bed and looked out the window to see where they were going. That's when I spotted him."

"Who?" Randi asked impatiently.

"I'm getting to it!" D.C. stomped his foot with frustration. "There was a man in a car parked right across from the museum. He had a pair of superpowerful binoculars, and he had them trained on the museum's entrance."

Randi felt a spark of excitement. "Could you tell what he was watching?"

"No," D.C. said. "But he was sitting there pretty much the whole time you guys were gone. Whatever he was looking at must have been pretty interesting."

Randi looked up at Gigi. "We had to have walked right past him!" Randi said. "I can't believe neither of us noticed anything."

"Hold on, guys. I think I might be able to solve the mystery," Gigi said. "Earlier this year, a pair of red-tailed hawks built a nest in one of the windows on the front of the building. This whole neighborhood was lousy with bird-watchers for months. I gotta say, it was a little creepy to walk outside and find two dozen people standing in the middle of the sidewalk with their binoculars focused across the street."

"But this is November," D.C. replied, sounding skeptical. "Don't birds lay their eggs in the spring? The hawk babies must have hatched and flown away by now."

"The nest is still there." Gigi pointed out the window. "Look at the second window from the right on the second floor. See those twigs sticking out?"

D.C. squinted into the sunshine. "Yeah," he said, his face falling. "I see it. But I swear, the guy didn't look anything like a bird-watcher. He was wearing a black leather coat. He seemed like some kind of gangster to me."

"Welcome to Brooklyn," Randi said. "Half the people here look like gangsters."

"That's not true." Gigi put a hand on D.C.'s shoulder. "You know what, D.C.? It's awfully early for bird-watchers. Maybe the guy *was* some kind of criminal."

"You think?" D.C. asked, sounding hopeful.

"It's possible," Gigi said, though Randi could tell she was only humoring the boy. "I'll tell you what. I'm pretty good friends with the superintendent here. He has security cameras

watching the front of the building. I bet if I ask nicely, he'll let us take a look at the footage from the last few days. Who knows? Maybe we'll catch our gangster doing something more exciting."

"That sounds awesome!" D.C. said. "Can we go now?"

"Absolutely not, young man," Gigi said, doing an impressive impersonation of Colonel Taylor. "Breakfast comes first. Then we must discuss our schedule for the rest of the day. A little bird told me there's a martial arts tournament in town."

CHAPTER EIGHT

STUNT DOUBLE

"No answer?" Randi asked.

"Nope." D.C. handed Randi's phone back to her as they followed Gigi down the sidewalk toward the site of the tournament. "It just goes straight to my dad's voice mail."

"He's probably busy," Pudge offered.

"Yeah." D.C. sounded unconvinced.

"Maybe it will be better this way," Randi assured him. "Now you get to surprise your dad!"

D.C. managed a weak smile. "I just hope he's glad to see me."

"Are you kidding?" Gigi asked. "Who wouldn't be glad to see a kid-sized ninja like you? Now, hurry up! We're almost there."

D.C. nervously reached under his coat and tightened the belt of his black *dobok*. He'd let out the hem of the *dobok*'s pants, but they were an inch too short and his bare ankles were red from the cold. Then his fingers adjusted the headband holding back his unruly thatch of hair. When Randi had first met D.C., he'd worn the headband every day—not to keep his hair under control but to cover the hearing aid he wore in his ear. Since they'd solved their first case together, D.C. had stopped hiding his hearing aid. But now the headband was back—and Randi wasn't happy to see it.

Randi crossed her fingers for D.C.'s sake. She hoped his reunion with his father was everything he hoped it would be. Then she turned her attention back to her surroundings. Gigi was leading them through a neighborhood filled with old factories, workshops, and warehouses. There was a faint stench of sewage in the air. According to Gigi, it came from the canal that ran through the area. As soon as she mentioned the canal, Randi noticed that a short blue bridge lay just ahead of them. The wooden boards of the deck creaked as they clomped across.

The slate-gray surface of the canal was like a mirror. When they stopped to gaze down at the calm waters, Randi could see the four of them staring up at themselves.

"The canal is kind of pretty," Pudge said when the sun hit the surface and turned a patch of oil into a glittering rainbow.

"Yep," said Gigi. "And completely disgusting. Whenever there's a big rainstorm in New York, the sewers fill up and they have to let sewage out. This is where they do it."

"So that smell . . . ," Randi started to say.

"It's the real deal," Gigi told her.

"This is where the tournament is being held?" D.C.

marveled. "Next to a canal filled with . . . poo?"

"Aside from the poo, it's a really cool neighborhood," Gigi assured them.

Two blocks from the bridge, they found the entrance to the warehouse where the tournament, or *she-hahp*, was being held. The space inside was massive—it stretched for as far as the eye could see. The floor was covered with a giant gray rubber mat with bright orange squares. The squares were the rings where tournament participants would be going head-to-head, foot-to-foot, and fist-to-fist. Everywhere she looked, Randi saw people of all ages dressed in Tae Kwon Do uniforms. It was, in her opinion, as close to heaven as she would ever get.

"It said online that my dad's judging the male sport *poomsae*. His group is fifteen- to seventeen-year-olds," D.C. said. "So look for teenagers."

"What's a *poomsae*?" Gigi asked.

"It's a sequence of Tae Kwon Do moves," Randi explained. "It's for training purposes, but putting the moves together can be an art. You're supposed to go through the moves very quickly but with perfect control and precision. Look over there. A kid's doing one now." She headed to a corner of the room where a boy was practicing a *poomsae* made up of punches and kicks. A small group of judges was watching. One of them in particular seemed to be really enjoying the show.

"Excuse me, sir," D.C. said when the performance had

finished. The man turned to face him, and D.C. bowed.

"What can I do for you, son?" he asked in a Southern accent so thick that you couldn't cut it with a chain saw. Randi tried not to stare. The man was extremely good-looking. He was in his midthirties, she estimated. His dark blond hair was cut very short—almost military style—and he had a set of twinkling green eyes. He looked better in a Tae Kwon Do uniform than anyone else in the room.

"I'm trying to find Hector Cruz," D.C. said. "He was supposed to be judging the *poomsae*."

"You got your days switched around," said the man. "He's here tomorrow."

"Oh," D.C. said. His chin fell to his chest.

"You fight, son?" the man asked D.C.

"Yes, sir."

The man gave D.C. a good once-over. "You look like you're right about twelve or so."

D.C. smiled. It was the first time anyone had ever guessed his age correctly. Because of his size, people usually thought he was much younger than he actually was. "I just turned twelve."

"Well, when you come back tomorrow, be sure to wear your regulation white uniform. I can't put you in the ring with a black *dobok* on."

"Thanks for the offer, sir. But I'm not signed up for the tournament. And I don't have enough money for a new *dobok*."

"Don't make a difference," the man said. "There's a table

selling *doboks* by the front door. Tell 'em Jake said to give you one."

"I probably shouldn't compete," D.C. said. "I have some health problems."

The man named Jake frowned. "Like what?"

"Asthma."

Jake looked unimpressed. "I had it too when I was your age. Tae Kwon Do helped me kick it. Anything else?"

"This," D.C. said, showing the man his hearing aid.

"Son," Jake said, with an arched eyebrow and a shake of his head. "There's a boy here with one arm and a girl who's completely deaf. As long as that hearing aid doesn't get in the way of your kicks, I can't see it causing too many problems. And as for signing up, I'm running this show, so I can put you on the list for tomorrow. As long as you give me your name."

"D.C. D.C. Cruz."

The man held out a hand. "Nice to meet you, D.C. My name is Jake Jessop."

Pudge lit up. "Jake Jessop? *The* Jake Jessop?" He sounded almost breathless with excitement.

"Dunno if I'm the one you're thinking of, but I've never met another," said Jake.

Randi and Gigi both stared at Pudge as the boy began frantically searching through his backpack. Finally, he pulled out a Sharpie and thrust it at the man.

"Can I have your autograph? Please?"

The man laughed. "Not sure I'm used to this kind of treatment. What would you like me to sign?"

Pudge rifled through his backpack but couldn't come up with a suitable piece of paper. "How about my backpack?" he asked.

As the man signed, Gigi stepped forward. "Pardon me for asking," she said sheepishly. "Are you famous?"

"No," said Jake, turning a bit red.

"Are you joking?" Pudge nearly shouted. "He's the best stunt man in Hollywood. Whenever you see a movie where some big shot actor is doing martial arts, it's almost always *this* guy who's doing the moves for them!"

"That's amazing!" Randi cried.

"I can't believe I just shook your hand," D.C. said, looking down at his palm.

"These kids sure know how to butter a guy up," Jake joked to Gigi.

Another judge tapped Jake on the shoulder.

"Oops. Looks like it's time to get started. Come back tomorrow, D.C. Cruz," he said. Then he gave Gigi a quick wink. "And be sure to bring your friends."

To celebrate meeting a celebrity, they ate pie for lunch at a sweet little restaurant they'd discovered near the warehouse. Gigi and Randi both had slices of peach. D.C. would have gone for "anything but apple," but ended up settling on a slice of "salty honey." Pudge ate a slice of all five of the pies available.

"You sure you want to do that?" Gigi had asked when she heard his order.

"Yup," he'd answered. "Way I see it, I'm never going to have a chance like this again."

"You know there's a pretty good reason why your parents would never let you eat five slices of pie in one sitting," Gigi said.

"Yup," Pudge had responded. "My dad says his rules are for my own good. They're supposed to keep me from getting in trouble. But you know what, Ms. Daly? I think I'd like to make some mistakes. There are a few things in life a guy like me should figure out on his own."

"Well put," said Gigi. "That's the best excuse for eating like a pig that I've ever heard. Be my guest."

Randi watched in amazement as Pudge ate every crumb. He didn't even seem to enjoy the last couple of slices, but he forced himself to keep chewing and swallowing. When the last bite had been consumed, he lay down on the restaurant's bench.

"I don't think I'm going to be able to walk back to the subway," he announced.

"I should think not!" Gigi said. "That's why I called a cab ten minutes ago. He's waiting for us outside."

"Arrrgh." Pudge groaned as the three of them helped him to his feet. "I'm never eating pie again!"

"I bet you won't," Gigi said. "Please try your best not to

throw up until we get back to the apartment. It would be cruel to ruin pie for the cabdriver, too."

When the taxi pulled to a stop in front of Gigi's building, she handed Pudge the keys to the apartment. Without saying a word to anyone, he leaped from the car and sprinted for the elevator.

"I really hope he makes it in time," Randi said.

"Me too," said Gigi. "'Cause in my house, there's only one rule: You spew it, you clean it."

D.C. and Randi were still laughing when they reached the building's landing. Suddenly D.C. went silent. He tugged gently on the back of Randi's shirt and subtly gestured toward a group of men who were cramming luggage and boxes into one of the elevators.

"That's the watcher!" he whispered in Randi's ear.

"The *who*?" she almost asked. Then she noticed the binocular case atop one of the bags. The man D.C. had seen watching the museum through binoculars seemed to be moving into Gigi's building.

There were three men, and there wasn't a swatch of black leather among them. They were wearing regular clothes. Khakis, sneakers, T-shirts, and Yankees baseball hats. *Too regular*, thought Randi. *And all of it new*. The clothes were pristine, and the sneakers didn't have a scuff on them. More interesting, the baseball hats hadn't been broken in. The bills were as flat as they would have been in the store.

Two of the men were serious types, with posture and hair-cuts that suggested they might have once been in the military. Their impressive biceps bulged as they heaved the boxes. The third was tall and thin, with curly black hair and an impressive nose. He smiled nervously at Randi and her friends.

"Moving in?" Gigi inquired casually.

The two burly men stood up. Randi took note of the boxes they'd been moving. They contained enough kitchen equipment to stock a restaurant. And all of it appeared to be brand-new.

"I am," said the man standing closest to the elevator. "My friends are here for the weekend to help me be settled." His manner was polite but not friendly. Something about it made it perfectly clear that he wasn't in the mood for socializing. And who said *be settled?* Randi wondered.

Gigi didn't seem to get the man's message. "Welcome to Brooklyn," she said, holding out a hand and flirting with aban-don. "I'm Georgia Daly. But everyone calls me Gigi."

The man hesitated. "I'm John."

"And who are your charming friends?"

"Bob and Jim," he said quickly with a note of irritation in his voice. He pushed up his shirtsleeves, exposing the part of a tattoo on his forearm. It looked like the bottom half of a beetle.

The curly-headed man stepped forward and shook Gigi's hand. "It is a pleasure to meet you." He spoke with a thick German accent.

The man with the tattoo who called himself John did not seemed amused. As soon as the handshake was over, he stepped between Randi's aunt and the German man. "Now, please excuse us. We have a large van to unpack."

"Of course!" Gigi trilled. She pressed a button, and the doors to the building's second elevator opened. "Good luck with your move!"

As soon as the elevator doors closed in front of them, Gigi began tapping away at her smartphone while D.C. immediately lost his cool. "Did you see him? That was the guy!"

"I know," Randi said. "And you were right. There's something weird about him and his friends. Did you see their clothes? None of them knew how to wear a baseball hat. They hadn't even broken in the brims. The tall one spoke with an accent, too. I don't think they were American."

"The one with the curly hair was German. The other two were Russian," Gigi announced, looking up from her phone. "But Brooklyn is filled with people from other places. Their accents aren't what make me think they're up to something."

The kids stared at the small blond woman. "What was it that made you suspicious?" Randi asked.

Gigi grinned. "The tattoo on the main guy's arm." The elevator stopped. Gigi stepped into the hall, and the kids poured out behind her.

"The bug tattoo?" D.C. whispered, following Gigi to the door. She put a finger to her lips as she opened the apartment door. Then she ushered them inside and quickly closed the door behind them.

They found Pudge lying on the living room sofa. One arm was wrapped around his belly. He had the other arm thrown over his face.

"Did you make it?" Randi asked.

"I made it," Pudge replied.

"Did you see the guys downstairs in the lobby?" D.C. asked.

"What guys?" Pudge groaned.

"The man I saw spying on the museum is moving into the building. He's got two friends with him. We talked to them, and Gigi thinks they might be up to something!"

Pudge sat up, looked disgusted with himself. "You guys got to talk to a bunch of crooks, and I wasn't there? I swear. I'm never touching a piece of pie ever again."

"You still haven't told us how you know about tattoos," Randi said to her aunt.

"The head guy has a tattoo of a beetle," Gigi said, bringing Pudge up to speed. "A scarab beetle. Right after medical school, I worked at an emergency room at a hospital in Brighton Beach, another part of Brooklyn. There's a big Russian community there. And one time, a guy came in with multiple bullet wounds. We had to cut him out of his clothes, and when we did, it turned out his entire body was covered with black tattoos. There were skulls and cats and ladies and knives. And I distinctly recall seeing a scarab beetle on the man's arm. One of the nurses at the hospital told me that they were jailhouse tattoos. In Russia, prison inmates often give themselves home-made tattoos. Every tattoo has a special meaning, and together they tell a story about their owner."

"What does a scarab beetle mean?" D.C. asked.

"I just looked it up," Gigi said, flashing her phone's screen at them. "It's a good luck symbol that's used by professional thieves."

"May I see?" Randi asked, putting her hand out for Gigi's phone. It was feeling way too good to be true. Randi had a hunch that Gigi was exaggerating—making the situation seem more thrilling than it was. But when Randi looked down at the screen, she found an image of a scarab tattoo that looked a lot like the one on the forearm of the man they'd met downstairs. The photo was on a website devoted to Russian prison tattoos.

D.C. gasped. "Those guys downstairs are thieves?"

"The beetle is evidence that one of the men *may have been* a thief," Randi said, trying to play the voice of reason. "We have no proof that any of them were ever criminals."

"Nope," Gigi said. "But I think I know how to get that proof. There's only one apartment in the building that's empty right now—the one directly below this one. That's got to be where the guys were going with all of those boxes."

"Great!" D.C. said. "We can stake out the hallway down-stairs."

"Or listen in at their door," Pudge added.

"That would be dangerous—not to mention unnecessary," Gigi said. "We can eavesdrop without ever leaving this apartment. Let me show you a little trick my sister taught me."

Randi watched Gigi hurry off to the kitchen. She returned in seconds with four plain glass mixing bowls. She handed one to each of the kids and kept one for herself. "It's not very high-tech, but it works like a charm."

"What are we supposed to do with this?" Pudge asked, turning the bowl over in his hands.

"Find a vent," Gigi said, pointing at a metal heating grate on the floor. She dropped down to her knees and placed her bowl upside down over the vent. Then she pressed one ear to the top of the bowl. "Nothing," she announced.

"You almost had me going," Randi said with a laugh. "I thought that was actually going to work."

"It will," Gigi said. "Conversations from downstairs travel through the heating ducts. The bowl magnifies the sound. There are two reasons I might not hear anyone. Either no one down there is talking—or they're in another room. Pudge, check the rest of the vents in here. D.C. and Randi, try the kitchen."

They all rushed off, some with more enthusiasm than others. Try as she might, Randi just couldn't get excited. Gigi was trying too hard to keep them entertained.

When Randi reached the kitchen, she put the bowl on top of the floor vent, the way Gigi had showed them. Then she placed her ear against the bottom of the bowl. Suddenly, she heard two men talking. The voices were soft, but perfectly clear. Still, she couldn't understand a word they were saying. The men downstairs were speaking in Russian.

"Hey, guys," she called out to her friends. "I got something."

Everyone rushed into the kitchen and took their turns listening through the crude microphone. D.C. and Pudge were captivated. It didn't matter that they couldn't understand a word they were hearing.

"Does the apartment downstairs have the same layout as this one?" Randi asked.

"It's identical," Gigi said.

"Then why are those guys hanging out in the kitchen?" Randi wondered. The kitchen was the one room in the entire apartment without a view of the museum across the street.

"Maybe they like to cook," D.C. said.

"Well, I don't," Gigi announced. "So if we're on a stakeout, we're going to be ordering dinner in tonight."

CHAPTER NINE

THE RETURN OF GLENN STREET

Randi dreamed she was swimming in a pool filled with warm caramel. Its heavenly fragrance surrounded her. She licked some off her fingers and savored the divine flavor. But then the gooey substance began to harden. It was getting more difficult for Randi to move her limbs. As much as she struggled, she couldn't free herself. She was sinking into the caramel, trapped like a fly in honey.

When Randi woke with a gasp, the sweet smell of caramel was still in the air. She followed the scent to the kitchen, expecting to find Gigi baking some kind of treat for breakfast. Instead, she nearly stumbled over Pudge and D.C., who were huddled together by the vent on the floor.

"Did you hear that?" she heard Pudge whisper.

"Yeah. They were speaking in Russian again," D.C. replied.

"Aren't they *ever* going to say anything English?" Pudge groaned.

"Why would they speak in English? They're *Russian*!" Randi

said, squinting in the bright morning sunlight that was pouring in through the window. She felt tired and grumpy. "Do you and D.C. ever speak to each other in Japanese? Or Spanish? Or Esperanto? Of course not. What are you two doing, anyway?" she demanded.

D.C. yawned. "That smell woke us up," he said. "We think it's coming from downstairs. The men were moving stuff around in the kitchen all night and now they're making something."

"Sure. It's called *breakfast*," Randi said. "And what's the point of eavesdropping on a bunch of guys who are speaking a language you can't understand?"

"Wow. Somebody woke up on the wrong side of the bed," D.C. muttered.

"Nobody said you have to help," Pudge told her. "But it's hard to hear them when you keep talking."

"Fine," Randi growled. "You two waste your time. I'm going out for a walk."

Randi went back to her room and threw on the clothes she'd left draped across a chair. She really was in a terrible mood. As she stomped toward the front door, her aunt emerged from her bedroom.

"Heading somewhere?" Gigi asked with a yawn.

"Out," Randi told her.

"Okay. I'm taking the boys back to the tournament around one," Gigi said. "Want to meet us there?"

"No," Randi told her. "I just want to be alone."

She expected an argument from her aunt. Instead, she heard, "All right, then. Have fun!"

All right, then. Have fun? As the elevator descended toward the lobby, Randi repeated the words in her head. What happened to *Where are you going?* or *When are you going to be back?* or *I don't think it's a good idea to stay up all night listening to men speaking Russian?* Gigi didn't believe in rules. But sometimes when it came to D.C. and Pudge, Randi thought, rules came in handy.

Randi stomped outside and headed south. The chilly air helped calm her down. But she was angry, and what bothered her most was that she couldn't figure out *why*. Waking up to find two boys camped out in her room was annoying, but it shouldn't be enough to send her into a tizzy.

It was the listening post, Randi realized. Gigi said Randi's mom had used it to spy on the neighbors. Randi had been to the apartment a thousand times. Why hadn't anyone ever mentioned it before? And why hadn't anyone ever told her that her mom had been such a wild child? It was like there was a big part of her mother that Randi had never been allowed to see.

Randi had walked almost half a mile before she realized the streets were unusually quiet. Only a couple of cars had driven past. And most of the houses she passed seemed empty. But a few on every block were bustling with activity. It was Thanksgiving, she realized. The thought turned her anger into a deep, dark sadness. She remembered the last Thanksgiving she'd spent with her mom. Olivia-Kay Rhodes had been ill, so Herb had cooked the turkey that year. It was dry and tasteless, but Randi would give anything to have another bite of it now.

And before she knew it, she was looking up at the building where that dinner had taken place. Her old home looked exactly the same as it had the day she'd left Brooklyn. A red-brick town house three stories high, it would have looked just like the other houses on the block if Randi hadn't known all the things that made it special. Only she and her father knew that the sour cherry tree growing in the tiny front yard had been planted by Olivia-Kay Rhodes the year Randi was born. Or that the chip in the second stair of the stoop had been made the Christmas morning that Randi had wrecked her first scooter. (The accident had left its mark on Randi, too—a crescent-shaped scar on her left hand.) Or that the top of the stoop was where Randi's mom would stand and wave every morning when Randi set off for school.

Randi knew the building's every secret. And yet she'd known so little about the woman who'd raised her there. Randi sat down on the stoop. She could feel the tears welling up in her eyes.

Then a sound from next door caught her attention. An

elderly couple, the Jacobsens, owned the house. Each year, they spent Thanksgiving with their son in Connecticut, and judging by the house's dark windows, this year was no different. And yet someone seemed to be standing in the dark alcove beneath the stoop. All of the town houses on the street had a half-hidden door that led to the ground floor. And when any houses on the street got robbed, it was always that door that the burglars used.

Randi rose from the step and quietly made her way to the sidewalk. She could see the figure clearly from there. It was a young man wearing a military-style parka, with its hood pulled up over his head. She couldn't see what he was using to open the door, but she suspected it wasn't a key. Randi felt in her pocket for her cell phone. But she didn't pull it out. The man at the door could be a nephew or a friend of the Jacobsens. Randi needed to eliminate a few possibilities before phoning the police. So she donned her most effective disguise—cute little girl.

"Hey, mister!" she called out to the man at the door. He jumped at least a foot in the air and dropped the shiny metal tool he'd been using to crack the lock.

"It's a kid," he muttered to himself. He pushed his hood back and tried to look respectable. He was in his midtwenties, Randi estimated. With dark brown hair and an enormous nose that would be easy to pick out in a police lineup. "Yeah?" he asked.

"You staying at the Schalanskys' house?" Randi asked, purposely using the wrong name and seeing if he took the bait. If he didn't correct her, he didn't belong there.

"Yep," he said. "That's right."

"Would you tell them my sister has kidnapped their cat again? She's been dressing it like a baby and pushing it around in a stroller. My parents think it's cute, but I know animal cruelty when I see it. The Schalanskys need to come and rescue it as soon as they get back."

The young man's brow furrowed. He was too nervous to laugh. "Sure, I'll tell them," he said.

"Thanks!" Randi said and skipped down the street. As soon as she was out of sight, she ducked behind a tree in a nearby front yard and dialed 911.

"Nine one one, what's your emergency?" asked the operator.

"I have a four-five-nine in progress at 239 Bergen Street. Young male Caucasian approximately twenty to—"

"Excuse me?" the operator broke in. "Is this a joke? How old are *you*?"

"What difference does it make?" Randi snipped. In the old days, she would have remembered to disguise her voice. She'd fallen out of practice living in Dullsville, Tennessee. "There's a man breaking into the house at 239 Bergen. I used to live next door, and I know for a fact that the owners are always out of town this time of year."

The operator hesitated. "All right," she finally huffed.

"I'll send a car over. Your name is coming up on caller ID as Miranda Rhodes. Is that correct?"

"It is."

"Well, Miss Rhodes, if this is a crank call, I'm going to be having a chat with your mom and dad."

"Knock yourself out," Miranda said. "My dad's name is Herb Rhodes. Want his number?"

"*The* Herb Rhodes?" the operator scoffed. "The man who writes those Glenn Street books? Young lady, this had better not be a joke. Do you know you can get in a whole heap of trouble calling nine one one for nothing?"

Randi bristled, but she managed to keep her temper. It wasn't the first time she'd been a victim of age discrimination. "This isn't a prank, ma'am," she replied calmly. "And as far as I know, there's no age requirement for being a concerned citizen. I'll be waiting on Bergen Street for the police car. Thank you for your assistance."

Randi hung up and rushed back to the scene of the crime. If the burglar got away before the police arrived, the whole situation was going to get messy. Randi stationed herself behind a rhododendron bush in a yard across the street from the Jacobsens' house. Soon she saw a figure pass in front of a window on the second floor. The burglar was ransacking one of the bedrooms. Within a minute, she spotted him again on the third floor. *He's fast*, she thought. *He knows what he wants and he knows where to find it. This isn't the first house he's robbed.*

And to make matters worse, the NYPD seemed to be taking its time. Randi's ears perked up at the faint sound of a siren in the distance—then her heart sank a little when it quickly faded away. She heard a second cop car with a wailing siren speed down a neighboring street without even pausing.

Randi was about to place a second call to 911 when the door on the ground floor of the Jacobsens' house opened a crack. The burglar scanned the sidewalk for witnesses and then emerged with a black trash bag slung over one shoulder. Randi wasn't about to let him get away.

"Hey!" She jumped out from behind the bush and rushed across the street.

The burglar froze.

"You know, trash day isn't until Tuesday," Randi said in a voice that her mother had called *little miss bossy pants*. "If you leave that bag out on the sidewalk, the Schalanskys are going to get a big fine."

"Then I guess I better take the bag with me," the burglar grumbled. "Thanks for the advice, kid."

He lugged the bag toward a beat-up van that was parked down the street. Randi knew that once he was inside, he was as good as gone. She could have memorized the license plates. Or snapped a picture with her phone. But that wasn't Randi's style.

"Hey!" she called out again when he put the bag down to open the van.

"Get lost, kid," the guy snarled.

"Why don't you make me?" Randi told him, assuming a combat stance.

"Are you kidding? Okay, fine," said the burglar, taking a menacing step toward her. "I didn't want to . . . *oooffffff*."

Randi's foot had slammed into his stomach. The burglar dropped to his knees, and Randi landed a perfect chop to the side of his neck. Two lightning-fast moves and the man was down for the count. Quickly, Randi unwound the scarf from her neck and secured the man's arms behind his back.

She was just finishing the final knot when the police rolled up.

"What the heck . . . ?" The first officer hopped out of the car. "What's going on here?" He clearly hadn't been expecting to see a twelve-year-old girl hog-tying a full-grown burglar.

The commotion had brought a few neighbors out on their stoops. Randi saw one with a camera aimed in her direction. She stood up to greet the two cops.

"I'm sorry, officers," Randi said. "This man just robbed a house on this street. He was about to make an escape, so I had to perform a citizen's arrest."

"You did this all by yourself?" the first cop asked. "What are you, *eleven*?"

Randi tried not to roll her eyes at the insult. "I'm twelve, sir, and a black belt in Tae Kwon Do."

"Come over here and take a look at this," the second cop called out. He'd opened the bag that the burglar had dropped after Randi kicked him. Inside, there were two laptop

computers, a tangle of jewelry, and three small paintings. "The guy's van is full of stuff, too. Most of it's gadgets and gold. Guy's been busy. Looks like he hit a whole bunch of houses this morning."

"Nice work, kid." The first cop gave Randi a congratulatory thump on the back. He was tall and thin, with a wide smile and hair almost as red as hers. She probably would have liked him if he hadn't introduced himself by insulting her age. "What's your name?"

"Miranda Rhodes."

"I'm Officer Cody," said the first cop. He pointed to his partner, a shorter, older man with curly black hair. "He's Officer Jackson. Where do you live, Miranda Rhodes?"

"I used to live down the street," Randi told him. "But now I live in Deer Creek, Tennessee."

"Lot of burglars to catch down there in Tennessee?" Officer Cody asked with a devilish grin.

"Not nearly enough," Randi replied.

"Well, maybe you should consider coming back." Officer Jackson had come over to join them. "Crime rate's been going up in this neighborhood. Used to be a vigilante who kept a pretty tight rein on things. Called himself Glenn Street after the character in those detective books. But he seems to have disappeared. We haven't heard a peep from him in about six months."

"From *her*," Randi corrected him. "Glenn Street was a *her*."

"Oh yeah?" Officer Cody asked as if he was just playing along. "If you knew *her*, where'd she go?"

"She moved to Deer Creek, Tennessee," Randi said. "But I hear she may be moving back."

CHAPTER TEN

SHOW-OFF

The call couldn't have come at a worse time. Randi was sitting in the backseat of a squad car, listening to the constant stream of announcements on the police radio. Officers Cody and Jackson had insisted on giving her a lift back to Gigi's house, since their backup officers arrived and hauled the thief to the station. Randi pulled out her phone and saw a way-too-familiar number appear on the screen. She didn't want to answer, but she knew it would only make him worry. Her best option was to take the call—and get off quick.

"Hi, Dad," she said.

"How are you, princess?" he asked, using the nickname she hated the most. "Having fun in Brooklyn?"

"Tons," Randi told him. "Can I call you back in a few minutes? I'm just . . ."

"*Armed robbery in progress. Bodega on southeast corner of Myrtle and Vanderbilt,*" the police radio blared in the background. Randi winced.

"Randi," her father said. There wasn't a drop of good humor left in his voice. "Was that what I think it was?"

Randi slumped down in the seat. "Yes," she admitted. Herb Rhodes had done a million ride-alongs with the NYPD while researching his books. He knew the sound of a police radio when he heard it.

"Miranda Jasmine Rhodes." Her father spoke slowly and pronounced every syllable. "Where are you right now?"

"In the back of a police car," Randi replied.

"Please hand this phone to one of the officers."

Randi passed the phone to Officer Cody. "It's my dad," she explained. "He wants to talk to you."

"Hello?" said the cop. "This is Officer Felix Cody of the New York Police Department. Who's this . . . ? Herb Rhodes? Wait a second. *The* Herb Rhodes? Oh man, I should have known! You know, you've got an amazing kid, Mr. Rhodes. . . . What . . . ? No, she's not in any trouble. In fact, she single-handedly foiled a burglary on Bergen Street this morning. . . . Pardon me . . . ? Yes, sir, I do know that she's twelve years old. . . . No, her aunt was not with her. We're taking her back to the aunt's house right now. . . . Yes, I can understand why she might be in big trouble. . . . Yes, sir, I will personally escort her to the apartment. . . . Yes, sir. You're welcome, sir."

Officer Cody handed the phone back to Randi. *You're in big trouble*, he mouthed. She took a deep breath before she put the phone back to her ear.

"I can explain . . . ," she started to say.

"No," her dad said. "You cannot, and I have no interest in hearing you try. It's Thanksgiving Day, so I probably won't be able to book a flight. But I promise you, Miranda Rhodes, I will be on the first plane that I can get to New York. I should never have let you visit Gigi on your own. She's not a good influence on a girl your age."

"Why?" Randi asked. She was getting angry, too. "What's wrong with Gigi? At least *she* doesn't keep secrets from me."

"What are you talking about?" Herb Rhodes demanded. "*What* secrets?"

"About Mom and all the cool things she used to do. You told me she was the inspiration for Glenn Street, but you never told me why. You kept it a big secret."

"And do you want to know why?" Herb Rhodes asked. "*This* is why, Randi. Do you have any idea how hurt you could have gotten just now? All you need to know is that your mother stopped playing detective because what she was doing was dangerous. And she had people who loved her and needed her."

"You mean . . ."

"I mean your mother stopped because she had *you*, Randi. Gigi didn't tell you that part, did she?"

"Mom may have stopped playing detective," Randi said, "but it didn't keep her from dying. Did it, Dad? You know why? Because *living* is dangerous."

There was silence on the other end of the line.

"I have to go," Randi told him. She could feel the tears in her eyes, and she didn't want to cry in front of the New York Police Department. "We just got to Gigi's building."

"Promise me there's not going to be any more detective work," Herb Rhodes said.

"No," Randi said. "I can't. Come and get me if you have to, but I'm not going to stop having fun. This is where I belong, Dad. You know it, too. I think that's what really scares you."

When Randi stormed into the apartment, she expected to find Gigi talking to her father on the phone. Instead, her aunt and the two boys were huddled around a computer in the living room. The smell of caramel still filled the house, but the others barely seemed to notice it.

"Hey." D.C. greeted her without looking up.

"Thought you wanted to be alone today," Pudge added. It was clear she'd hurt their feelings by stomping out.

"What he means is that we're glad to see you," Gigi said. "We've got some exciting news."

"Did my dad call?" Randi asked.

Gigi's brow furrowed. "Were you expecting him to call?" she asked.

It wasn't a straight answer, but it made Randi relax a bit. Maybe her father had come to his senses and decided not to call off his book tour. "I never know what to expect from Herb Rhodes. What's your big news?"

"The guys downstairs. We finally heard one of them talking in English," D.C. said. "We think he must have been on the phone. He said: *The delivery is due on Friday.*"

Randi plopped down on the sofa and put her shoes up on the coffee table. Mei-Ling would have had a fit if she'd seen Randi with her feet on the furniture, but Gigi didn't seem to mind. "That's your big break in the case?" Randi asked, feeling a little disappointed. "He just moved in. He might be having a couch delivered."

"Or maybe he was talking about *this*." Pudge turned the computer around to face Randi. On the screen was a story about the Brooklyn Museum's Fabergé exhibit. "We've been doing some detective work. Says here that the Imperial Eggs are being delivered by armored car to the museum on Friday night."

"And you guys think those men downstairs are planning to steal them?" Randi asked.

D.C. shook his head in exasperation. "What other explanation could there be?" he replied. "I saw one of the guys watching the museum with binoculars. Then he and two other guys end up moving in downstairs. Turns out one of them has a thief's tattoo. Now we hear them talking about a 'delivery' on Friday night. He's gotta be talking about the Fabergé eggs. I think we should contact the police."

"You could, I suppose." Randi didn't want to be a killjoy. Nothing would have pleased her more than having a heist to foil. Still, she worried that the boys were getting way too excited way too fast. "But here's another scenario. Let's say a guy who likes bug tattoos rents an apartment in the building. He stops by the day he's supposed to move in and sees a rare hawk in a nest on the building across the street. Because he's moving, he happens to have his binoculars in the car. He takes a look. Later that day, his friends help him move some of his stuff in. He calls the movers to see when his furniture is coming. They tell him he can expect the delivery on Friday. Sound possible?"

"Yeah," D.C. admitted.

"What do you think?" Pudge asked Gigi.

Gigi took a moment to consider. "Have you ever heard of Occam's razor?" she asked.

"What's a razor got to do with this?" D.C. asked.

"It's not a *razor*," Gigi said with a laugh. "It's a principle that states that the simplest explanation is usually the correct one. In other words, as much as I'd like to think there are a bunch of egg thieves downstairs, Randi is probably right. Odds are it's just a bunch of guys waiting for a furniture delivery."

"Darn," Pudge said. "I was really looking forward to some excitement."

"Are you joking? This is *New York City*!" Gigi told him. "There's a thrill around every corner. In fact, as I recall, we already have some exciting plans today."

"We do?" Randi asked.

Gigi sighed dramatically. "Did everyone forget about the tournament? And look what I happened to pick up yesterday on our way out." She grabbed the large handbag she'd been carrying and pulled out a pristine white *gi*, which she presented to D.C. "I think it's time for one of us to get dressed."

The warehouse by the Gowanus Canal was even more packed than it had been the previous day. It took them ages to squeeze through the crowds as they made their way toward the junior competitions.

"Excuse me. I'm looking for Hector Cruz," D.C. said to an official who was preparing to judge a match.

"You just missed him," the man said. "He said had to get home for Thanksgiving dinner with his family."

"His family?" D.C. repeated. His whole body seemed to crumple a little. Randi stepped forward and threw an arm around the boy's shoulder.

"I'm sorry," the man said, seeing the impact the news had on the boy. "Hector might be back tomorrow if you need to speak with him."

"Thanks for your help, sir," Randi said when D.C. couldn't answer.

He had started to sniffle when someone with a Southern accent called out, "There you are!" Jake Jessop was waving them over to the mat where the twelve- to fourteen-year-old boys were competing.

"Hi, Mr. Jessop," said D.C., perking up a bit.

"Welcome back," Jake said. Then he looked over and gave Gigi a wink. "Glad to see all y'all. You ready to have some fun, D.C.? I see you came prepared." He pointed to D.C.'s regulation Tae Kwon Do uniform.

"I'm not sure I'm feeling up for it," D.C. admitted, staring down at his feet.

"That's too bad, 'cause I asked your dad if it was okay to give you a good workout today. Get you ready to show off tomorrow."

When D.C. looked up at Jake, a tear ran down his cheek. "My dad knew I was coming today? And he didn't stick around to see me?"

Jake Jessop squatted down a bit so he could look D.C. in the eye. "I know for a fact that he wanted to, but he couldn't. He told me he was looking forward to catching up with you tomorrow. Now, get in this ring and let me see what you can do." He opened up the gate in the black fence that separated the competition area from the viewing area and let D.C. pass through. "Hey, Kevin," he called out to a boy who looked about thirteen. "I got you a sparring partner."

Kevin was a full head taller than D.C. He was already wearing a helmet and padded vest, and he smirked smugly as he waited for D.C. to be strapped into protective gear. Then they took their places at the center of the mat, and Jake signaled for the match to start.

Kevin was good, but not good enough. D.C. bounced around the mat like a dynamo, never letting the older boy land a punch or a kick. Instead, he waited for Kevin's energy level to drop. That's when he pummeled him with punches and twice knocked the boy to his knees. Then D.C. spun around, leg high in the air. His heel made contact with Kevin's chin. The thwack that came with the kick was so loud that Randi was surprised to see Kevin's jaw remained intact. The boy was fine, but the fight was clearly over.

Jake whistled appreciatively from the sidelines. "Well, I guess talent does run in the family. Your dad teach you those moves?"

"No, sir," D.C. said. "I haven't seen my dad in three years. My friend Randi taught me."

A cloud passed over the man's face when he heard about D.C.'s dad. "Well, I'm impressed," Jake said. "You think you might be able to show off some of those moves on Saturday? I get to pick the best from each division to take part in an exhibition at the end of the tournament. You want to represent the twelve- to fourteen-year-old boys?"

"You're picking *me*?" D.C. asked.

"Yup," Jake confirmed.

D.C.'s excitement seemed to fade in an instant. His looked down at the mat and touched his headband to make sure his hearing aid remained hidden. "You don't have to choose me just because you feel sorry for me," he said.

"Feel sorry for you?" Jake Jessop let out a whoop of a laugh. "Boy, I'm *jealous* of you. I'm not interested in doing anyone any favor. I picked *you* 'cause you're the best I've seen."

CHAPTER ELEVEN

CAVIAR DREAMS

The cab shot over the Brooklyn Bridge toward the glittering island of Manhattan. In the backseat, Randi and Gigi were dressed in chic black dresses. D.C. and Pudge were both wearing sleek suits with festive orange ties, which had magically appeared in their bedrooms while they were cleaning up before dinner.

It was Thanksgiving night, and everyone was in the mood to celebrate. After a long chat with a very persuasive Gigi, Randi's dad had reluctantly decided not to call off his book tour. D.C. would soon be showing off his skills at a Tae Kwon Do tournament. Pudge hadn't followed a rule in more than thirty-six hours. And Gigi couldn't stop giggling to herself about the special dinner she'd arranged for the evening.

"We're going to a restaurant in Manhattan?" D.C. asked.

"Looks that way, doesn't it?" Gigi responded mysteriously. "But I'm not saying anything else. I told you guys it was a surprise. Hope you aren't disappointed, but I'm pretty sure there won't be any turkey this Thanksgiving."

"That's okay," Pudge said. "I always thought turkey was kind of fowl."

"But you sure do enjoy cheese," Randi ribbed him.

"Cheese!" D.C. cracked up. "Good one!"

"Hardy-har-har," Pudge responded, and then started laughing for real.

The taxi sped up the FDR Drive on the east side of Manhattan until they reached Midtown. Soon, they were traveling across Fifty-Seventh Street through the city's ritziest shopping district. The cab stopped in front of a narrow building with a bright red awning and three dancing gold bears on its facade.

"The Russian Tea Room," D.C. said, reading the words written on the awning.

"Surprise!" Gigi said. "I hope you're in the mood for caviar!"

Even Randi gasped the moment she stepped inside. The interior of the Russian Tea Room was one of the most spectacular things she had ever seen. The walls were green and decorated with phoenixes gilded to match the golden ceiling. The plush banquettes that lined the walls were a brilliant cherry red, and the chandeliers appeared to be decorated with red Easter eggs. As the maître d' guided them toward their table, Randi couldn't help but stare at the exotic dishes the other guests were eating. Red soup, escargot, and tiny black fish eggs in crystal bowls.

Randi had never even seen caviar before—and now she might actually get to try it.

The party of four slid into a banquette and each was handed a menu. Gigi immediately laid hers down on the table.

"Your attention, please. Before we kick off this special Thanksgiving dinner, there are a few things I'd like to say." She paused to smile at each of them in turn. "First, I'd like to thank you for being here with me tonight. It's been so much fun having you in New York. You're a fabulous group of ninjas, and it makes me very happy to know that Randi has such good friends."

Then Gigi trained her gaze on Randi. "You're the only family I have left, Miranda," she said. "And you're the best niece I could have ever asked for. My Thanksgiving wish is that I get to spend a lot more time with you in the future."

Randi hugged her aunt. "I really hope I can make that wish come true." She'd been thinking about it all afternoon. There was no reason to return to Deer Creek. Her dad was back on the book tour circuit, and he'd never be home. Amber-Grace and her popular girl posse were determined to get Randi expelled from school. And if the incident with the burglar that morning had taught Randi anything, it was that Brooklyn was where she belonged.

"Really?" Gigi whispered.

Randi nodded. What could be better than living with a

rich, wonderful aunt who loved a good adventure and didn't believe in having any rules? Her friends would always be welcome to visit. And she could probably talk Gigi into hiring Mei-Ling, too.

"We'll talk about it later," Gigi said, squeezing Randi's hand. "What about you, Pudge? Are you thankful for anything?"

Pudge had been cramming bread rolls and butter into his mouth. He chewed vigorously and swallowed until there was just enough room in his mouth for his tongue to form words.

"No sisters. No parents. No chores. No rules. No Thanksgiving green bean casserole. This has been the best vacation *ever*."

"I'm glad you're having a blast." Gigi laughed. "D.C.? Seems to me that you've got a lot to celebrate tonight. Want to tell us what you're thankful for?"

"I'm thankful for Jake Jessop," D.C. said with no hesitation. "He is, hands down, the coolest guy in the entire world."

"That's funny," Gigi replied with a mischievous wink. "I'm thankful for Jake Jessop, too. What do you say, kids? Should we invite Jake over for dinner on Saturday after the Tae Kwon Do exhibition?"

"Yeah!" they cried in unison.

"Then consider it done," Gigi said. "Now, let's get some food in our bellies. I'm thinking we should start with a little bit of that."

Gigi pointed to a waiter who was carrying a tray with what

appeared to be a gigantic bowl of caviar on top. A large spoon-ful of the ebony fish eggs could cost three hundred dollars, and there had to be ten times that amount on the tray. Wondering who could have ordered such a pricey appetizer, Randi fol-lowed the waiter to a corner of the restaurant with her eyes.

He delivered the dish to a dashing silver-haired gentleman with a tan that suggested he'd walked right off a yacht. A pink silk tie and matching pocket square added a dash of whimsy to his crisp navy suit. He thanked the waiter for the caviar, but made no move to eat it. He was too busy examining a small vase filled with wildflowers that sat in the center of his table. There were daisies and daffodils. Pansies and irises. From a distance, each flower looked absolutely perfect.

A second man was sitting across the table from the gentle-man, his back facing Randi. He reached out and pulled the cav-iar toward himself as if he didn't plan to share. Randi couldn't see his face, but she could tell that the second man's table man-ners were a bit rusty.

"Excuse me," Randi mumbled to Gigi and her friends. "I'm going to wash my hands before we get started."

She headed in the direction of the table where the two men were seated. There was something about the pair that didn't seem right. Over the years, Randi had learned to trust her instincts. As Glenn Street always said, *A hunch is your gut telling you something that your brain doesn't know yet.* Whenever Randi's gut decided to say something, she tried to listen.

"Sweetie, I don't think the restroom is over there," her aunt called out, but Randi pretended she hadn't heard.

As she drew closer to the two men, the sound of Russian being spoken met Randi's ears. Though she couldn't understand a word, it was easy to tell that the men came from different walks of life. The gentleman spoke softly while the other often grunted in reply. Just as Randi was about to get a glimpse of the grunter, a third man magically appeared. He wasn't a waiter. Judging by his smarmy smile, he was some kind of lackey.

"May I have them bring you anything else, Prince Gorchakov?" he asked the man in the suit.

"No, thank you, Yuri," the man replied without looking up. He continued to examine the flower arrangement in the center of the table, turning the vase slowly and brushing the blooms with his fingertips.

"Tell them to bring more vodka," the man across the table ordered. He reached out an arm and grabbed an empty bottle that sat in the center of the table. As he thrust it toward the waiter, his shirtsleeve rode up, revealing the bottom half of a scarab beetle. It was the watcher. "So you like?" He gestured toward the flowers.

The refined older man smiled. "Oh yes," he said. "They're absolutely marvelous. Thanks to these beauties, it won't be long until I'm rearranging my wine cellar." Then he plucked a daffodil out of the arrangement and popped it into his mouth.

Randi froze, unable to comprehend what she had just seen. Before she had a chance to turn around, the smiling lackey was standing over her.

"May I help you?" he inquired in a voice that wasn't nearly as friendly as the one he had used to address the prince.

"I'm just looking for, uh, the ladies' room," Randi stammered.

"You might want to look the *other* way," the man announced, pointing toward the opposite side of the restaurant. "There's nothing for you back here." ☠

☠ Go to Appendix C to complete the Ninja Task!

CHAPTER TWELVE

PRINCE OF DARKNESS

"He's not a real prince," Randi said. She was sitting at the desk in Gigi's living room, her eyes skimming over one of the many articles she'd found online. "Says here that he gave himself the title."

"You can do that?" D.C. asked.

"Guess so," said Gigi.

"Then from now on, I want you guys to call me Prince Pudge." The boy started to cackle, then held his belly and curled up into a ball on the living room couch. "Arrrggghhh," he groaned miserably.

"I told you not to eat two orders of beef stroganoff," Randi said, feeling very little sympathy for the tall, thin kid whose growing belly looked like it might burst out of his jeans. "The way you've been shoveling food down your throat, Pudge, you're gonna finally live up to your name."

"But those noodles were sooooo good." Pudge moaned.

"And my mom and dad never let me eat whatever I want when I'm at home."

"Yeah, well, maybe your parents know something you don't," D.C. said without shifting his gaze away from the computer screen.

"You think?" Gigi added with a twinkle in her eye.

"I think it's crazy that we're wasting time talking about Pudge when we could be talking about the Prince of Darkness," Randi said.

"You mean the devil?" D.C. asked in a hushed voice.

"No, that's just what they call 'Prince' Andrei Gorchakov," Randi explained. "He's not the devil, but they say he's a pretty bad guy. He grew up in one of the Russian communities in Brooklyn, and now he owns a chain of expensive pastry shops. The police say he's the head of an organized crime syndicate, but they've never been able to prove it. They don't even know for sure where he lives."

"He sounds like a supervillain," Gigi noted. "Evil on the inside, fancy on the outside."

"A supervillain who enjoys eating daffodils," D.C. added.

"I almost forgot about the flower!" Gigi said. "The weirdest part is that daffodils are poisonous. And I'm pretty sure they don't taste very good, either."

"Extreme eating doesn't exactly fit Gorchakov's profile," Randi said. "This is a guy who's known for his expensive clothes and fast cars. And art dealers say he's put together one of the best collections of Russian art in the world. They think he keeps it in a secret museum somewhere. But nobody has ever seen it. He keeps the art just for himself."

"And let me guess," Pudge chipped in. "He likes Fabergé eggs."

"Nope. He *loves* them," Randi said. "He's bought every egg that's been auctioned off in the past ten years. But there aren't that many Imperial Eggs—and they don't come up for sale very often."

Gigi sighed dramatically. "Such a shame. What's an egg-loving supervillain to do?"

Randi swiveled around in her seat. "I think we all know the answer to that question," she said. "Andrei Gorchakov hired those men downstairs to steal the eggs he couldn't buy."

The next morning, they were up before dawn. D.C. was stationed by the heating vent in the kitchen, listening to the men downstairs. Pudge was by the window with binoculars, keeping an eye on the museum across the street. Randi was in position in the building's lobby in case the men made their move. And Gigi was across the street, sitting on a bench in front of the museum, drinking coffee and pretending to read the newspaper.

"Ninja One, this is Ninja Two." D.C.'s voice came through Randi's walkie-talkie.

"Hello?" she heard Gigi respond. "Is that Pudge?"

"*I'm* Ninja One," Randi told her aunt for the third time that morning. "Pudge is Ninja Two and *you're* Ninja Four."

"Sorry!" Gigi said. "Still getting the hang of this!"

"What's up, Ninja Two?" Randi asked D.C.

"It's gone quiet in the apartment downstairs," Pudge reported. "And I just heard a door shut. I think they're heading your way."

"Thanks for the heads-up," Randi said, slipping into an alcove by the mailboxes. She heard one of the elevators moving. A minute later, the doors opened and two men stepped out. Both were wearing navy-blue uniforms. One of them was the watcher. The other was his Russian colleague. The German was still upstairs.

Randi watched as they marched through the lobby and out the front door. "Ninja Three and Ninja Four, subjects are on the move. They're dressed as security guards. I'm going to give them a head start. Don't let them out of your sight."

"Roger that," said Pudge.

"This is so exciting!" whispered Gigi. "I see them now! They're approaching the pedestrian crossing on Eastern Boulevard. Now they're waiting for the light."

It was time to move. Randi pulled the hood of her coat over her head and hurried through the apartment building's double glass doors. The men were already halfway across the street. There was no doubt about it—they were on their way to the museum.

Smart, Randi thought. *The museum is probably hiring extra security for the exhibit, so the foxes got a job in the henhouse.*

Both of the men were carrying large duffle bags. Randi could tell from the way the men held them that the bags didn't weigh very much. *Can't be weapons inside,* she said to herself. *Those bags must be where they'll stuff the loot.*

She tailed them from a distance as they headed straight on Washington Avenue toward the back entrance of the museum. Randi stayed close to the fence that circled the museum's grounds. Strong gusts of wind lifted piles of dead brown leaves in the air. The tree branches that hung over the sidewalk creaked and groaned. One of the men checked over his shoulder. Randi stopped short and hoped her black coat would make it hard for them to see her among the shadows.

At the back of the museum, employees were filing in and out of the service entrance. The nighttime staff was trading places with those who worked during the day. Randi waited until the two men were inside before she rushed up to a woman who was coming out the door. Randi held her cell phone up for the woman to see and put on her cutest little-girl voice.

"Excuse me, ma'am! My dad works here. My mom and I just dropped him off and he left his phone in the car! Is it okay if I give it to him?"

"What's your dad's name?"

"Oscar Gruber," Randi said, pulling a random name out of

her head. "He just started on Friday. He's a security guard for the new exhibit."

The woman gave Randi a once-over. Once she'd concluded that a girl Randi's age couldn't pose much of a threat, she held the door open. "Make it quick, kid," she said with a yawn. "It's not Bring Your Daughter to Work Day."

"Thanks!" Randi trilled. She squeezed past the woman and entered the bowels of the museum.

The door slammed behind her, and Randi found herself inside a long empty corridor. Security cameras mounted on the walls scanned every last inch of it. The two thieves must have gone into the men's locker room. Its door lay just to Randi's right. She didn't dare follow them inside—but she couldn't hang out in the hall, either. She had to keep moving or she'd be kicked out in minutes. It would be harder for anyone to find her, she figured, if she was upstairs with the art. The two men would be heading to the egg exhibit eventually. Instead of trailing them, she might as well meet them there.

A stairwell lay ahead. According to the museum's website, special exhibitions were usually located on the fifth floor. The eggs hadn't arrived yet, which meant security wouldn't be in full force. So Randi scrambled upstairs and opened the door. She stepped into a room that was painted jet-black. There was no furniture, just tall glass boxes. Inside the display cases, empty shelves were covered in black velvet. She'd found the room where the eggs would be shown. It had been designed so that nothing would distract from the eggs' beauty. Which meant there was nowhere for Randi to hide.

"Excuse me, little girl?" a haughty voice called out. "Just what in the blue blazes do you think you're doing?"

An angry lady in a prim tweed suit was marching in her direction. Randi rushed for the stairwell exit, but the door wouldn't open. There were no other exits, no escape routes. She was trapped.

Randi instantly recognized the two police officers who'd come to collect her from the museum. They were the same guys who'd driven her home after she'd foiled the burglary on Bergen Street.

"And look who we have here," said Officer Cody, elbowing his partner. "Told you it was gonna be her. Pay up." He put his palm out, and the other man slapped a twenty-dollar bill into it.

"I should have known better," Officer Jackson grumbled. "You're on a roll, and I haven't won a bet in weeks."

The small, grimy room where Randi was being held had no windows and little furniture. There were two rickety folding chairs, a flickering light fixture that hung from the ceiling, and a table with one leg that was shorter than the other three. Officer Cody grabbed one of the chairs, spun it around, and straddled it. "What's up, Miranda Rhodes? There are a couple of kids loitering outside the museum who look like they're worried sick about something. They friends of yours?"

Randi said nothing.

"You better start talking or we'll have to take you in. Let's see if you can make this story as good as the last one."

Officer Jackson leaned against the wall. "We thought you were one of the good guys," he teased her. "Now we're called out to pick you up for trespassing? Didn't take you long to turn to a life of crime."

The interrogation could have been worse. But inside Randi was seething. She didn't like to be needled.

"I wasn't trespassing," she corrected them, doing her best to sound as serious as possible. "I was tailing two men who, I believe, are planning to steal the Fabergé eggs that are arriving here at the museum tonight."

"Egg thieves, eh?" said Officer Cody, winking at his partner. "I knew this was gonna be good. The guys at the station are going to eat this up."

Randi scowled before she continued. "Three men just moved into the apartment below my aunt's. Two of them are Russian. One of them has a tattoo of a scarab beetle on his forearm. I suppose you know what that means."

"That the dude likes bugs?" Officer Jackson asked.

Randi sighed at his ignorance. "It's a jailhouse tattoo. In Russian prisons, every piece of body art has a meaning. A scarab beetle tattoo means the man is a thief."

"Or it could just mean that the man digs bugs," Officer

Cody pointed out. "My girlfriend's got a ladybug tattooed on her wrist."

Randi chose to ignore the comment. "Last night, I saw the man with a tattoo having dinner with the Prince of Darkness, Andrei Gorchakov."

"The devil's name is Andrei?" Officer Jackson laughed.

"No, she's talking about that gangster. You know, the one from Brighton Beach who owns those fancy pastry shops," Officer Cody said, sounding a little more interested in Randi's story. "So where does a twelve-year-old kid go these days to see a guy like Andrei Gorchakov eating dinner?"

"The Russian Tea Room," Randi said. "My aunt took us there for Thanksgiving."

"I've always wanted to give that place a try," said Officer Jackson. "How was the food?"

"It was fantastic." Randi huffed. It was getting harder and harder to keep her cool. "But that's not the point. Andrei Gorchakov likes Fabergé eggs. But the most precious eggs— the Imperial Eggs—almost never come up for sale, so he's decided to steal a dozen or two. He hired the men I was fol-lowing to rob the museum!"

"That's a pretty serious accusation," said Officer Jackson. "You got any proof other than a bug tattoo and a fancy dinner?"

"Isn't that enough to make the guy a suspect?" Randi argued.

"It makes him interesting; that's all," Officer Cody said. "So far the only crime that's been committed here is trespassing. And you're the one who committed it."

"I just told you that millions of dollars in Fabergé eggs are about to be stolen, and you're talking about *trespassing*?" Randi scoffed.

"Today it's trespassing; tomorrow it could be robbing 7-Elevens. You know what they call trespassing, don't you? They call it the gateway crime," Officer Cody managed to say with a straight face.

"They do *not*," Randi argued.

"You know what?" Officer Cody asked his partner. "I bet I know who can settle this argument."

"Who?" asked Officer Jackson, playing along.

"Herb Rhodes. Think I should give my favorite author a call?"

A chill trickled down Randi's spine. If the cops called her dad, the jig would be up and the fat lady would start to belt out a tune. He'd already threatened to come get her once. Another conversation with the NYPD, and Herb Rhodes would be on the next plane to New York.

"Fine," Randi said. "I give up. You don't need to call my dad. I was playing a game, and I let my imagination get out of control. But look how easy it was for me to get inside the museum. Don't you think they could use some extra security?"

If Randi couldn't catch the burglars herself, she could at

least make sure that there were enough cops on hand to collar them once the crime was committed.

"I'll talk to the boss," Officer Cody said.

"Promise?" Randi asked.

"You're awfully big for your britches, but you've got my word," the cop assured her. "Though the security here is pretty tight already. Just between us, you're not the only one who's worried about the eggs. The lady in charge told us that Fabergé eggs have a habit of vanishing. So they've got their eyes on every inch of this museum. They saw you on the cameras the second you stepped through the door. How do you think we got here so fast?"

"Wait a second. Eggs have been vanishing?" Randi asked. "What are you talking about?"

Officer Jackson gave his partner a disapproving look. "He shouldn't have said anything," he told Randi. "It's time for you to let the grown-ups here do their jobs. They don't need any help from fifth graders."

"I'm in the *seventh* grade," Randi said between clenched teeth.

"I don't care if you're in the *tenth* grade," Officer Jackson said. "Your investigation is over."

"Let us take it from here," Officer Cody added. "Otherwise we'll have to call your father. And I sure would hate for the legendary Glenn Street to get grounded."

~ ~ ~ ~

"Well, it's obvious what our next step should be," Gigi said when Randi was released into her custody by the police for the second day in a row.

"It is?" Randi asked, feeling miserable. She was banned from the museum. The police had promised more security at the exhibit, but they hadn't exactly bought her story. In fact, the entire precinct was probably having a good laugh at her expense. The next step, as far as Randi was concerned, would be crawling under the nearest rock. D.C. and Pudge didn't seem much happier. Only Gigi remained optimistic.

"Of course it is!" she insisted. "The four of us did our jobs. We uncovered evidence that a crime was about to be committed. We identified the culprits and alerted the authorities. So what if they didn't believe you? Tonight, when the eggs go missing, they'll be pounding on our door."

"You think?" D.C. asked.

"Absolutely," said Gigi. "Our next step? Wait for the burglars to come back to the building with the stolen eggs in tow. And then prepare to be heroes!"

CHAPTER THIRTEEN

THE VANISHING EGGS

After the morning's excitement, the next ten hours felt impossibly dull. The museum across the street seemed perfectly peaceful—and the apartment below Gigi's stayed silent. At eight o'clock in the evening, the ninja detectives finally got their first little thrill when a van from Channel One pulled up in front of the museum and a reporter hopped out. *Something newsworthy must have happened*, Randi thought. She, Gigi, and the kids waited breathlessly, expecting the police to follow shortly behind.

A few white delivery trucks came and went. Then they heard the men downstairs return home from work. But the NYPD never arrived. At ten o'clock, Pudge was the first to fall asleep. Then D.C. passed out, and Gigi wandered off to bed shortly after. Soon Randi was the only one awake in the apartment. From time to time, sirens outside made her rush to the window. But the police cars always sped past. A helicopter flew over the museum, its spotlight briefly illuminating the building's dome. Then it buzzed off into the distance. When the clock struck midnight, Randi knew the delivery must have taken place, but somehow the eggs hadn't been stolen.

Randi refused to go to sleep. Instead, she sat at Gigi's desk, trawling the Internet for information. Back at the museum, Officer Cody had let it slip that Fabergé eggs had a habit of vanishing. Randi expected to uncover news reports of heists or armed robberies. She found nothing of the sort. What she discovered instead was far more interesting. In less than two years, three Imperial Eggs had literally disappeared under *very* mysterious circumstances.

The first egg had vanished from an auction house in New York City. A dazzling creation worth more than ten million dollars, it had arrived one evening with a battalion of guards. Early the next morning, there was a small fire in the building. In less than a minute, the sprinkler system had extinguished the blaze. But when the excitement was over, auction house employees discovered that the egg was gone. Despite the fact that the auction house was filled with expensive art, nothing else had been taken.

Police assumed that whoever had set the fire had also stolen the egg. But the room from which the egg was taken had no windows, and a guard had been stationed outside the room's only door. The guard would have been the obvious suspect if it hadn't been for the security cameras that were trained on the spot. They clearly showed that throughout the fire, the guard had never moved an inch. No one else could have gotten inside the room. The egg had simply vanished.

The second egg had gone missing from a small private plane that was transporting a shipment of art from Switzerland to Saudi Arabia. The egg's owner had personally supervised the packing of his treasures and watched them be loaded onto the plane. Somewhere over the Red Sea, the plane had experienced engine troubles. The pilot managed to make a water landing, but the plane and everything else inside it had sunk. Three weeks later, a recovery crew brought the plane to the surface. The art was wet, but not permanently damaged. The wooden crate in which the Fabergé egg had been packed was perfectly intact. None of the nails had been removed. But when the crate was opened, the owner discovered it was completely empty.

The third and last missing egg had belonged to an aged Belgian countess. The egg had been a gift from one of the woman's many admirers—though she couldn't remember which one it had been. For years, the egg had sat on the vanity in her bedroom, alongside a fortune in jewels. One morning, a toilet in the bathroom above the woman's chamber overflowed. While the servants scrambled to fix the flood, the countess refused to leave her bed. She later swore to the police that she had never once left the room. The ceiling was still dripping when a maid began to clean up the vanity and realized that the countess's prized egg was missing. There was no sign that the

"Okay," Randi said, though she hadn't had a glass of milk in at least five years.

"Is there something on your mind, kiddo?"

"Why didn't you call today?" Randi asked, surprising herself. "Is it because you're mad at me for busting that burglar?"

"Hold on one moment, sweetheart," Herb Rhodes said with a sigh. She heard him making excuses to his dinner companions. He was taking the conversation outside. "No, of course not. When I talked to your aunt on the phone yesterday, she told me that I overreacted. I'm sorry, princess. I wanted to give you a little space. That's why I didn't call today. I don't want you to think I'm always breathing down your back."

Randi grimaced. If her father only knew what she'd been up to in the last twenty-four hours, he'd lock her in her bedroom for the rest of her life.

"You don't have to worry about me so much, you know," she said, trying to convince herself at the same time. "I've told you a million times that I'm old enough to take care of myself."

"I know. It's just . . ." He cleared his throat. "It's just that you're the most precious thing in the world to me, Randi. If something were ever to happen to you . . ."

Randi could hear the fear in his voice, and she didn't enjoy knowing that she was responsible for it. "Nothing's going to happen to me, Dad," Randi tried to assure him.

"You're twelve years old and you think you're invincible," Herb said. "I don't expect you to understand."

house had been burgled. A diamond necklace and a pair of
earrings that she'd left on the vanity had been left untouc[

Randi scribbled notes as she read. The disappearance[
had several things in common, she noted. A distraction of so
sort had preceded each one. Plenty of people had the opp[
tunity to handle the eggs in the hours before they vanishe[
But there were never any suspects because no one had had t[
chance to steal them. The Imperial Eggs were simply there on[
moment—and gone the next. A reporter joked that the thie[
had to be an invisible man. Who else could steal an egg from
a guarded chamber, a moving plane, or an occupied bedroom?
Randi knew there had to be a more logical explanation.

She felt for the phone in the pocket of her jeans. Mysteries
like this were her dad's specialty. Randi was about to dial his
number when she remembered the argument they'd had on
Thanksgiving Day. Any mention of missing Fabergé eggs was
bound to make him suspicious. She hated keeping secrets from
her father, but sometimes it was for his own good.

Herb Rhodes answered after the very first ring. "Randi?
Everything okay? It's past midnight your time."

"Everything's fine," she assured him. She could hear tinkling glasses and laughter in the background. Her father was
out to dinner. "I just couldn't sleep."

"Oh good." He sounded relieved. "Ask Gigi to make you a
glass of hot milk. When I can't get to sleep, that usually does
the trick."

"Understand? Understand *what*?" The word had annoyed her. One of the many problems that came with being twelve was that no one expected her to understand anything.

"That you're responsible for the people who love you," her dad told her. "It's your job to protect them whenever you can. But it's just as important that you protect yourself. Because the worst thing that could possibly happen to someone who loves you would be to *lose* you."

He was trying to tug on her heartstrings, and it didn't seem fair. She hadn't called her dad to fight, but Randi could feel the anger rising within her. "If I'm so darn important to you, why are you off on a book tour right now?"

"Excuse me?" Herb Rhodes asked. "What does my book tour have to do with this?"

"Everything! Don't you see? This trip meant everything to me, but you didn't even consider my feelings," Randi said. "I thought we were going to go visit Mom together. But then you left us again to go talk about books. Just like you used to do back when Mom was alive."

Herb Rhodes cleared his voice twice before he spoke. "Have you been to the cemetery to see your mom yet?"

"No," Randi said. "But when I do, I'll be sure to send your regards."

The left side of Randi's face was blazing hot. She opened her eyes to find the sun streaming in through the living room windows. She'd fallen asleep facedown on Gigi's desk. In an instant, Randi was out of her seat and standing at the window. The museum across the street was dark and the street below deserted. If anything had happened during the night, she'd managed to sleep right through it.

Randi dropped back down into the chair and quickly called the *New York Times* up on the computer screen. The front-page stories covered a scandal in the mayor's office and a baboon that had escaped from the Prospect Park Zoo. There was no mention of stolen eggs.

Gigi glided out of her bedroom in a floor-sweeping silk dressing gown. "Nothing happened?" she asked with a yawn.

"Nope," said Randi.

Gigi didn't seem to mind. "Then I guess our little adventure is over," she said as if little adventures were a dime a dozen. "Sure was fun while it lasted." She lay down on the sofa and flipped on the television. The local news channel appeared on the screen.

A female reporter was interviewing the woman who had chased Randi out of the Fabergé exhibit. According to the caption on the screen, her name was Beverley Winthrop, and she was a curator at the museum. Behind the two women, men wearing white gloves were opening crates. For a moment, Randi was confused. Then she realized that the footage the news channel was playing had been recorded inside the museum the previous night.

"Turn it up!" Randi cried.

"We've been informed that there was a security incident earlier today," the television reporter said. "Can you tell us more about that?" She thrust the microphone at the other woman and waited for a response.

Beverley Winthrop turned an unflattering red. "I would hardly call it an *incident*," she snipped. "A child entered the museum before official visiting hours. Security cameras tracked her movements throughout the museum, and she was apprehended right here in this room."

The reporter produced a professional-grade frown. "Surely any breach of security must worry you," she said. "Three Imperial Fabergé eggs have disappeared in recent years. Law-enforcement officials believe they might have been stolen, but the thieves remain at large. Are you satisfied that the museum is prepared to house two dozen priceless eggs?"

"Absolutely," Beverley Winthrop insisted. "In fact, after the child was taken into custody this morning, the NYPD agreed to provide additional security throughout the exhibit's run. There's no risk whatsoever of these eggs vanishing."

Randi grinned. Officer Cody must have made good on his promise and asked his boss to assign additional cops to the museum. Maybe that was the reason the eggs hadn't been stolen. The extra security could have convinced the thieves downstairs to call off the heist.

"Thank you, Ms. Winthrop," said the television reporter,

marking the end of the interview. She turned away from the frazzled curator and faced the camera with a wide smile. "The Fabergé Imperial Eggs have arrived at the Brooklyn Museum, and they're being unpacked as I speak. Each one is a remarkable work of art and craftsmanship. Together, the twelve eggs are estimated to be worth half a billion dollars."

The Channel One camera zoomed in on a man with a beard opening one of the crates in which the eggs had arrived. A sparkling oval rested in a nest of tiny foam beads. Made of gold and decorated with diamonds, the egg appeared to be a clock with a bouquet of white lilies sprouting from its top. The man carefully removed the egg, handling it as if it were made of spun air. The camera followed him as he gently placed the egg on a pedestal.

When he'd finished his work, the man glanced up at the camera. He quickly turned away, but for one fleeting moment, his full face was captured on film. And Randi's heart nearly leaped out of her chest.

"I swear I just saw the German guy from downstairs," she told Gigi.

On the television, the camera was panning across a dozen Fabergé Imperial Eggs that had already been removed from their crates. They were displayed on pedestals that stood on a long, velvet-covered table. The glass cases that Randi had seen when she broke into the exhibit were still empty.

"Why are the eggs just sitting out in the open?" Randi wondered aloud.

The reporter seemed to reply directly to Randi. "Some lucky celebrities and VIPs will be given a sneak peek of the Fabergé exhibit tomorrow evening. The mayor has invited a select group to see the eggs up close and personal—and discover the secrets within them. After the party, the miniature treasures will be placed in specially made display cases. And on Sunday morning, the Imperial Eggs will all be on view to the public."

"Maybe the thieves were scared off by the security," Gigi said, reaching the same conclusion that Randi had come to. "Looks like they must have missed their big opportunity."

Randi didn't answer. Her eyes remained glued to the television screen. Before the channel cut to commercials, she saw him. The man with the scarab tattoo was standing guard by the door to the exhibit. His face was as unreadable as ever. But somehow he didn't look like a man who'd just missed out on a big opportunity.

CHAPTER FOURTEEN

MOVING OUT

Randi was dreaming she was swimming through caramel again when a voice whispered in her ear.

"Can you help me?"

"Mmmrwwwaaa!" She sat bolt upright in bed, ready to attack the intruder.

"Randi, it's me!" D.C. cried, grabbing the wrist of the hand that had nearly punched him. His reflexes were getting faster and faster, Randi noticed. "I need your help!"

"What time is it?" Randi asked. After an uncomfortable night on the desk, she'd fallen back asleep in her bed. Even with the shades closed, her room felt as bright as the sun.

"It's noon," D.C. said. "The tournament exhibition starts in three hours."

He was nervous, and Randi could hardly blame him. It would be only his second time performing in front of a crowd—and his first time performing in front of his father.

"What do you need?" Randi wiped the sleep out of her

eyes. "Want me to practice with you or something?"

"No," D.C. said shyly. "I need you to help me do my hair."

"What?" Randi laughed before she saw the serious look on D.C.'s face.

"Jake said I couldn't wear a headband. Will you fix my hair so it covers this?" He tapped the hearing aid in his ear.

"Why do you want to cover it?" Randi asked, though she already knew the answer.

"My dad's going to be there," D.C. said. "I don't want him to know I still have it. I want to look fit and strong."

Randi's heart broke when he said it, but she didn't for a moment let on. She knew that D.C. blamed himself for his parents breaking up and his dad moving away. D.C. had been born premature, which left him with asthma and hearing problems. He thought his dad was disappointed to have been burdened with a sickly kid. If that was true, it was Hector Cruz's problem, Randi thought. It had nothing do with his amazing son.

"If you want to impress people, I wouldn't hide that hearing aid when we get to the tournament," Randi said. "I'd show it off instead. It's not proof that you're weak, D.C. It's a sign of your strength. You had to face a lot of challenges to get as good as you are. It was harder for you—and that's why you're more skilled than those other kids."

D.C. hung his head. "I don't think my dad will ever see it that way."

"Jake will," Randi said.

Those two words seemed to make all the difference. D.C. cracked a grin. "Maybe you're right," he said.

"Of course I am!" Randi exclaimed, falling back on the pillows. She could have used another hour of sleep. "I'm always right."

Overnight, the warehouse in which the Tae Kwon Do tournament was taking place had undergone a makeover. The mats were gone. There were no clusters of spectators and participants. There was only a single stage at one end of the building, with spotlights shining down upon it. The rest of the warehouse was dimly lit. Two thousand eyes were glued to the action taking place on the stage. Standing at its base, waiting for D.C.'s performance to begin, Randi scanned the crowd, looking for the man whose picture D.C. carried with him wherever he went.

"Any sign of him?" D.C. asked anxiously. An eight-year-old girl was performing an impressive series of kicks onstage. Her performance would be over soon, and an eleven-year-old boy was eagerly waiting on the stairs to take her place. When he was finished, it would be D.C.'s turn. Jake, Gigi, Pudge, and Randi were there, waiting to cheer him on. Hector Cruz was not.

Pudge tried to break the news gently. "I don't think your dad's here yet."

"He's not," Randi said. *And at this point, he might not want to*

show up, she thought. *I got a few things I might have to say to him if he does.*

"I'm sure your father's just stuck in traffic," Gigi tried to assure D.C.

"Or maybe he wrote down the wrong time," Pudge tried.

"Or maybe he's just a selfish jerk who needs a good punch in the nose," Randi said, earning an elbow in the gut from Pudge.

"That wasn't very nice," Gigi said, admonishing Randi for the first time ever.

Jake must have been watching D.C. grow increasingly worried, because he took the opportunity to step in.

"It wasn't nice what Randi said," Jake agreed with Gigi. "But it was true. And D.C. is strong enough to handle the truth." He squatted down in front of the boy and took D.C. by the shoulders. "I don't think your dad will be coming today."

D.C.'s lower lip started to tremble. "Why?"

Jake never took his eyes off of D.C.'s face. "Well, now, let's talk about that for a minute," he said. "Why do you think a father wouldn't see his son for three years? Or make an effort to go see his boy perform?"

Tears raced down D.C.'s cheeks. "Because he thinks his son is weak and worthless."

Randi could feel tears in her own eyes as well, and she wanted to hug the small boy.

"You're wrong, D.C. You're not the weak one," Jake said. "*He* is. Your father didn't come today because he's ashamed of how he's treated you, and he can't face up to it."

"You think?" D.C. asked.

"I *know*," Jake told him. "Look, fathers are just like everyone else. None of them are perfect. Good fathers make mistakes, too. Mine certainly did. But they own up to their mistakes. They don't hide from them. They try to fix them instead. If your dad was worth a darn, he'd have seized this opportunity to make things good with his son. Instead, he couldn't find the courage."

D.C. wiped his tears away with the sleeve of his *dobok*, and Randi was glad to see that no more arrived to replace them. She couldn't help thinking about what Jake had said. Her father had made his share of mistakes as well. No one could accuse Herb Rhodes of being perfect. For years, he'd spent more time with his books than he had with his family. But the move to Deer Creek had been his attempt at fixing that mistake. Randi had been the one who'd pushed him to start writing again.

"Now, get out there on the mat," she heard Jake order D.C. "Make it good, too. I got a couple of guys standing over there waiting to see what you can do."

He pointed to two hip-looking guys with chunky black glasses who were standing on the edge of the crowd.

"Who are they?" D.C. asked.

"Casting agents," Jake said. "I'm not just in town for the tournament. I'm filming a few scenes in Chinatown for my next film. And as it turns out, we need someone your age to double for the kid who's gonna star in the movie."

"And they're interested in *me*?" D.C. asked breathlessly.

"I told them you were the man for the job," Jake said. "So do your best not to prove me wrong."

D.C. started to argue. "I don't know if I can . . ."

"Son, after all you've been through in your life, I'd be real surprised if there's anything you *can't* do."

D.C. beamed from ear to ear.

"*And now*," they heard the master of ceremonies say over the loudspeaker, "*representing the twelve- and thirteen-year-old age group, Dario Cruz!*"

The performance had been a spectacular success. The crowd had *ooh*ed and *ahh*ed with every kick D.C. executed and every punch he threw. And when he'd ended with three perfect jump spin hook kicks in a row, the audience had roared with excitement. Even better, D.C. had landed the job of stunt double in Jake Jessop's next movie.

Now they were back at Gigi's house, gathered around the dining room table and feasting on six different kinds of takeout. The next day would be the ninja detectives' last in Brooklyn, and Gigi wanted to give them the kind of feast they'd never find back in Deer Creek, Tennessee. There were dishes from every corner of the world—Lebanon, Cuba, Malaysia, Argentina, and Sweden.

"When was the last time you ate goat?" she asked D.C.,

holding up a spoonful of chunky, delicious Cuban goat stew.

"Couple months ago," D.C. replied matter-of-factly, and the whole table laughed.

"What?" he asked, turning red. "Did you guys forget that I live on a farm?"

"I've eaten a few goats in my day, too," Jake said. "My mother back in Louisiana makes a mean Cajun goat curry."

"Is that where you live?" Randi asked. "Louisiana?"

"Part of the time," Jake said. "I travel around quite a bit. In fact, I'm thinking about spending a bit more time in Brooklyn." He cast a quick glance at Gigi, who blushed like a schoolgirl. Randi didn't need to be a detective to figure out there was something going on between the two of them.

"You won't be bored, that's for sure. It's nonstop excitement around here," Gigi said, moving the conversation along. "Why don't you guys tell our guest about the Russian thieves who live downstairs?"

"You got Russian thieves in the building?" Jake asked with a laugh. "That's a real selling point right there. Been meaning to bone up on my Russian. It's gotten a little rusty. My thieving skills could probably use a bit of work, too."

A long silence followed. Randi looked at Gigi. Pudge looked at Randi. D.C. looked at Pudge.

Jake's grin vanished. "What? Did I say something wrong? I was just kidding about the thieving. I've never stolen a thing in my life."

Gigi cleared her throat and set down her napkin. "Did you just say you understand Russian?"

"Yep," Jake said. "I learned it in the army."

Another long silence followed.

"Okay, now I'm confused," Jake said. "What's the big deal about knowing how to speak Russian?"

That's when everyone started to talk at once.

Jake pressed his ear to the top of the bowl. "Wow, this actually works," he said. "I can hear them talking downstairs."

He listened for almost ten minutes straight before he sat up.

"So what did they say?" Randi asked.

"Not much. They aren't exactly the most talkative bunch. But you'll be happy to know that you won't have to worry about them anymore," the stunt man told the group. "Sounds like they're moving out in the morning."

"Good," Randi said. "Let's hope this whole experience has turned them off of eggs for the rest of their lives."

Jake frowned. "Weird thing is, they didn't sound too depressed about it. In fact, I got the sense that they were taking something pretty valuable with them."

"But the eggs aren't missing. Do you think they could have stolen something else from the museum?" D.C. asked.

"With all that security?" Gigi responded. "Highly unlikely. They were probably just talking about their equipment."

"The museum is throwing a special party for VIPs

tomorrow," Randi said pensively. "I was worried that the thieves might try something then, but if they're leaving town in the morning, I guess they really have given up."

"Randi got the NYPD to station more officers at the museum," Gigi explained to Jake. "The extra security must have scared the crooks off."

Pudge threw his hands in the air and did his signature victory dance. "Another case closed. The ninja detectives are two for two!"

"Good job, everybody," Randi said. "Thanks for helping us out, Jake."

"My pleasure," he told the group. "I'm just grateful I got a chance to work with a real-life team of ninja detectives."

"I say this great news calls for something sweet," Gigi announced. "Want to help me get dessert ready?"

"Sure," Randi said, heading toward the kitchen.

"Actually, I was asking Jake," her aunt said. "He brought something for all of us to share."

"It would be an honor," Jake said, gathering the dishes that the kids had stacked and following Gigi into the kitchen.

Ten minutes passed and the two adults still hadn't emerged.

"What do think they're doing in there?" D.C. asked, staring at the kitchen door.

"Washing the dishes," Pudge joked, kissing the back of his hand.

"Hey!" Randi was about to set him straight when Jake came

out of the kitchen with a pastry box in his hands.

"So! You guys up for a culinary adventure?" he asked. "I picked up a special treat from my favorite Korean restaurant."

"*That's* the dessert you were just fixing?" Pudge teased, pointing at the package in Jake's hand. "It took you guys ten whole minutes to open a pastry box?"

"Don't be cheeky," Jake warned with a wink. He opened the box and set it down on the table. Stacked inside were what looked like waffles in the shape of fish.

"They're not actually *made* out of fish, are they?" Pudge asked.

"Nope. They're waffles with cream or red bean paste inside," Jake said.

"How'd they get them in the shape of fish?" D.C. asked.

"Duh," said Randi. "They used a fish-shaped waffle iron. I bet you could get an iron that makes waffles in any shape you . . ."

Her brain was suddenly whirling away so fast that her mouth couldn't catch up. The first thing she remembered was the powerful smell of caramel that had woken her up on Thanksgiving morning. Then the kitchen equipment they'd seen the men downstairs moving into the elevator. The poisonous daffodil that the Prince of Darkness had popped right into his mouth. And the way the man opening crates at the museum had handled the eggs inside with extraordinary care.

"Randi? Are you okay?" Gigi asked.

"The men downstairs stole the eggs," Randi announced. "They're moving them out in the morning. And if we don't have proof by the time they skip town, those eggs will never be seen again."

CHAPTER FIFTEEN

SWEET TEETH

It was five o'clock in the morning, and the sun still hadn't peeked above the horizon. The three ninja detectives and Gigi were standing in the dark by the living room window, watching as the men from downstairs finished packing a white van with boxes.

"Ninja One, come in, Ninja One." The voice came from the walkie-talkie in Randi's hand. Jake was sitting in his car, which was parked half a block from Gigi's building.

"This is Ninja One," Randi said. "Tell us what you've got, Daredevil."

"It's a white Ford van, license plate number TGD1652. It's carrying three men and twenty-four boxes of various sizes. I've taken pictures of the suspects and their cargo."

Randi jotted it down in her notebook. "Excellent work, Daredevil," she said. "You've been a great addition to the team."

"Thank you," Jake replied. "Any chance of me becoming an official ninja detective?"

"We'll see," Randi told him. "There's a test you have to pass first."

D.C. giggled in the background.

"Wow, you guys are tough," Jake said. "Okay, they're all in the van now. The engine just started, and . . . they're off."

Randi and her friends watched the van drive away. No one moved an inch until the vehicle's taillights had disappeared into the early-morning darkness.

Randi was the one who gave the word. "Time to rock 'n' roll. Jake, we're going in. Stay in position and keep an eye on the front door. Give me a shout if it looks like anyone might be coming our way."

"Roger that," Jake said.

The ninja detectives and Gigi crept down the hall single file. They had to move fast. Randi was convinced that the thieves had left incriminating evidence behind. But even that wouldn't make much of a difference if the crooks were able to skip town before the proof made it to the police.

They passed the elevator and took the fire stairs instead. Soon they were standing in front of the door to the apartment. Randi tried the knob. It refused to turn, so she dug into her back pocket and pulled out one of Gigi's old credit cards.

"Are you sure this is gonna work?" Pudge whispered.

"They left in a pretty big hurry," Randi said. "I doubt they took the time to lock the dead bolt. If the knob has the same kind of lock that Gigi's has, it should be a cinch to open."

She slowly slid the credit card between the crack and the door. The lock popped open.

"It was that easy?" Gigi looked both shocked and impressed. "I'll never forget to lock my dead bolt again."

Inside the apartment, a sickly sweet odor hung in the air. The living room was completely empty. The men had left nothing behind.

"What exactly are we looking for?" Gigi asked.

"I'm not sure, but I'll know it when I see it," Randi responded. She hadn't let anyone else in on her theory. It was too nuts for even the ninja detectives to believe without some solid proof. "Let's check out the kitchen."

The smell was even stronger inside the kitchen, which was as empty as the rest of the apartment. Fortunately, the men hadn't bothered to clean. A long island in the center of the room was sprinkled with a substance that had hardened into shiny splotches. The floor was covered with the same stuff, and the soles of Randi's sneakers stuck to the tile with each step she took. Randi wet a finger with her tongue, ran the tip across one of the splotches, and stuck it back into her mouth.

"Eeeew!" Pudge exclaimed with disgust. "Miranda Rhodes! Did you just do what I think you just did?"

"Relax," Randi said with a roll of her eyes. "It's sugar."

"That doesn't look like sugar to me," D.C. argued.

"Nope," Randi replied. "And that's the whole idea."

"I don't get it," Gigi said.

Randi needed to show them something more impressive than splatter. Then a bolt of inspiration made her fall to her knees. She crawled around the kitchen island, searching the tiles for something that the men might have dropped. And then she saw it. Trapped in a crack between two of the tiles was a tiny yellow flower. No larger than a baby pea, it was absolutely perfect in every way.

"Bingo," Randi said. "Take a look at this."

The others reluctantly got down on their hands and knees for a look at the tiny object that had fallen into the crack.

"It's a flower," Pudge said. He didn't sound terribly impressed.

"Looks like one, doesn't it?" Randi asked. "What if I told you it was made out of sugar?"

"I'd say you were nuts," D.C. said, reaching out to pick it up.

"Don't!" Randi shouted. She grabbed at his arm, but it was too late.

D.C. had plucked the miniature flower out of the crack. "Wow. You're right," he said. "It's not a plant. It's hard like . . ."

Suddenly, the flower shattered between his fingertips. He looked down at the tiny pieces and then up at Randi. "I'm so sorry!" he blubbered. "I'm so, so . . ."

"The damage is done. Stop talking and taste it," Randi ordered.

D.C. grimaced, then stuck his fingers in his mouth. "It really was made of sugar," he announced.

"But how is that possible?" Gigi exclaimed. "And what does it have to do with the stolen Fabergé eggs?"

"Don't you see? They made copies of the eggs—out of sugar," Randi said. "There are pastry chefs who can make almost anything out of sugar. It's called sugar sculpture. And what kind of businesses does Andrei Gorchakov own?"

"Pastry shops," Pudge answered.

"Yep. He must have hired a good chef to make the fakes. This flower looks just like one of the flowers on an Imperial Egg called Basket of Wild Flowers. It's one of the eggs in the Fabergé exhibit. The thieves probably came here with molds of the eggs they wanted to steal. Then they poured the sugar into the molds and painted the result to look like the real thing. Somehow, they managed to switch some of the eggs the day the delivery was made to the museum. Now they have the real eggs. The ones on display across the street are made out of sugar."

Randi's three companions gaped at her. Despite the desperate situation, Randi couldn't help but grin.

"How on earth did you figure that out?" Gigi asked. "And if you say, *It's elementary*, I'm going to kick you right in the rump."

"I kind of knew something was up when your apartment smelled like cooking sugar," Randi explained. "Then there was the daffodil that the Prince of Darkness ate. But it took those fish waffles that Jake brought for me to put the pieces together. I figured if you can make fish out of waffles, you could make eggs out of sugar."

"But why would the thieves use *sugar*?" D.C. asked. "Why not clay or something? Sugar eggs won't last very long, will they?"

"Nope," Randi confirmed. "Because sugar dissolves. And if the fake eggs happen to get wet, they'll melt. Remember I told you about the three Imperial Eggs that seemed to vanish into thin air? The authorities knew that someone must have stolen them—but at the time they went missing, there hadn't been anyone around to take them. But the eggs didn't disappear—they got wet and *dissolved*."

"It's brilliant," Gigi marveled. "You switch a real egg for a fake one. Then you arrange to make the phony egg disappear when you're not around. You won't be a suspect because you weren't at the scene of the crime."

"Exactly," Randi said.

"Wait," said D.C. "Is that why the men just left? They already stole the real eggs and left the fake ones behind. Now that they're gone, does this mean the sugar eggs at the museum are going to disappear soon?"

"Yep," Randi confirmed. "My guess is they'll disappear tonight. The news report yesterday morning said that the guests at tonight's VIP opening are going to get to see the eggs 'up close and personal.' I'd bet you a million dollars that the sprinkler system is tripped during the party. When the water hits the eggs, they'll dissolve. It will look like the eggs have been stolen, and everyone at the party will be a suspect. Meanwhile, the real thieves will have already made their escape."

"We've got to go to the cops!" Pudge urged.

"But D.C. squished our proof," Randi said. "The police will never believe me after everything that's happened. They'll think I'm just trying to cause more trouble."

"Maybe the thieves dropped something else on the floor," D.C. said.

"Everybody get down and start looking," Randi ordered.

"Ninja One, come in, Ninja One." Jake's voice squawked through the walkie-talkie hooked to Randi's belt.

"What's up, Daredevil?"

"There's a professional cleaning crew on the way up," Jake reported. "I pretended to be the superintendent and asked them where they were going and they told me apartment 6D. They've got a thug with them who looks like he might be packing more than a broom. You need to get out now!"

Randi shoved the walkie-talkie back in its holster. "Okay, guys. You heard the man. Let's beat it."

She ushered everyone out of the apartment and closed the door softly behind her. They had barely taken three steps down the hall when they heard the elevator arrive. Four men stepped out. Three were dressed in gray uniforms and carrying cleaning equipment. The fourth was wearing a tailored suit. The men stopped when they saw Randi and her friends. Standing shoulder to shoulder, they formed a solid barrier. There was no way around them.

"Excuse me," Gigi said politely.

The men didn't move. The one in the suit examined them with narrowed eyes.

"I didn't know kids these days used police-issue walkie-talkies," he said, pointing at the device in the holster attached to Randi's belt.

"They do when they're playing paintball," Randi replied in a chipper voice.

"That's our secret weapon," Pudge joined in. "Communication."

"Yeah," D.C. added. "We're the champions in our age group."

"I'm so proud of them," Gigi gushed. "And to think these little urchins had never had any weapons training before I adopted them last year. Would you like to see our family's trophy case? Our apartment is just at the end of the hall. I have videos, too!"

"Thanks, but no thanks," the man said, suddenly eager to make an escape. When he stepped aside, the ninjas and Gigi hurried toward the elevator.

"You sure?" Gigi asked.

"Never been more sure of anything in my life," the man replied as the elevator doors slid shut.

"Whew. That was close," D.C. said.

"Good thinking, guys," Gigi said. "Let's get home."

"Not yet." Randi hit the button for the basement.

"Why'd you do that?" Pudge asked.

"There's one other place where we might find some evidence," Randi announced. "Making those eggs must have been pretty messy. I'm betting there's something to be found in the trash."

The garbage room in the basement of the building was overflowing with identical black sacks. Finding a tiny shard of evidence would be like searching for a needle in a haystack.

"Today's garbage day," Gigi said. "The superintendent is going to start moving these bags out to the sidewalk soon. Then the garbagemen will come by to collect them."

Randi spotted a box of Latex gloves on a shelf by the door. She took out a pair for herself and then tossed the box to

Pudge. "Then we better get busy looking," she said.

"But how do we know where to start?" D.C. asked.

"Use your nose," Randi said. "See if you can find any bags that actually smell good."

Randi picked up the bag closest to the entrance and gave it a whiff. "Dirty diapers," she said, gagging as she tossed the bag to the side. "I think we can rule that one out."

D.C. lifted a sack up to his nose. "Holy moly, that's nasty," he announced. "Definitely kitty litter." The bag quickly joined Randi's.

"I guess it's my turn," Pudge said, looking at the bag in his hands. He gave it a sniff. "I think I'm gonna throw up. I'm pretty sure something died in there."

"Hey, guys," Gigi called out. "I've got something."

She turned a black garbage bag upside down, and a pile of sweet-smelling plastic wrap tumbled out. Randi got down on her knees and searched through the trash, hoping to find one tiny piece of what the men had been making. There were plenty of shards of a substance that looked like glass and tasted like sugar. But there was nothing she could take to the police. Then, at the bottom of the pile, she found a tag with several barcodes, a word spelled in the Russian alphabet—and three letters she recognized. JFK, the code for John F. Kennedy International Airport.

"What is it?" Pudge asked.

"Looks like a luggage tag," Randi said. "This must have

been on one of the men's suitcases when they flew into New York."

"Is it something we can use?" Gigi asked.

"I'd say so," Randi replied. "If the airline scans the barcodes, they can tell who the luggage belonged to, where they flew in from—and when they're flying back." ☠

_____

☠ Go to Appendix D to complete the Ninja Task!

CHAPTER SIXTEEN

CAT BURGLARS

Randi and Jake squatted at the base of the Brooklyn Museum. They were dressed in black from head to toe. Pudge and D.C. had both begged for the chance to escort Randi on the mission, but Gigi had refused to let either of them go. She wasn't going to let her niece set off on a dangerous operation without some adult supervision. So Jake Jessop ended up with the job.

"I can't believe I'm going through with this," Jake said softly, adjusting Randi's safety harness.

"Yeah, it's amazing what some guys will do for a girl," Randi joked in a whisper.

"Well, you are pretty darn persuasive," Jake told her.

"Ha!" Randi cackled before she caught herself and lowered her voice. "You and I both know that I'm not the girl I was talking about."

Jake Jessop turned bright red. "Sure you're up for this?" he asked.

"Absolutely," Randi replied.

"Okay then." The device he took out of his backpack looked like a thick plastic gun. Jake raised his arms and fired it as if he were shooting at the stars. A black rubber ball shot out of the gun, carrying a length of rope behind it. The ball hit a statue high above on the museum's wall, and the rope wrapped around its legs. Jake tugged on the rope to see if the hold was firm.

"Wow. I wasn't sure that would work," Jake said. He'd borrowed the device from the prop guy on his movie set. "I go first. When I get to the second floor, you can start climbing." He lifted a foot and put it on one of the building's marble blocks. Then, using the rope, he began to slowly walk up the side of the Brooklyn Museum.

There was no other way. Randi had made that much clear. With the VIP party taking place on the fifth floor, the museum was under heavy security. None of the ninja detectives (real or honorary) had a chance of making it through the door. A window was Randi's only option. Having played several ninjas and a handful of cat burglars, Jake was confident he could help her reach a window. There was no doubt that Randi would be caught soon after she got inside. But that didn't matter, as long as she managed to get her hands on one of the eggs first.

Jake gave her a thumbs-up, and Randi began to climb. It wasn't long before she realized that scaling the side of a building was harder than it sounded. Randi's arms were exhausted before she reached the second floor. Their goal was the fourth—just one floor below the exhibit. By the time she reached the third, her muscles were shaking and her hands were raw and sweaty. She could barely force herself to keep going. The hum of helicopters had just appeared in the distance when Randi lost her grip and plunged toward the earth.

The cord attached to Randi's safety harness broke her fall. The quick stop knocked the breath out of her—but she knew far worse would have happened if she'd hit the ground. Suddenly, she began to rise again, a few feet at a time. Jake Jessop had made it all the way to the roof. Randi could hear the grunts he made as he pulled her up. They grew faster and more urgent as the sound of helicopters drew closer and closer.

Randi jerked her head in the direction of the noise. Two NYPD choppers were heading straight for the museum, their searchlights sweeping nearby roofs. If the searchlight landed on Randi for even a second, the operation would be over. The cops in the chopper would radio the museum and have security guards waiting inside for Randi and Jake.

Jake kept pulling as the helicopters sped toward them like two angry hornets. Finally, Randi felt her body slip over a railing.

"Lie facedown next to the railing," he panted as he pulled up the rope they'd used to scale the side of the building. Randi flattened herself against the ground. When the last coil of rope

was over the side, Jake dropped to the floor. That instant, their side of the museum was suddenly lit like a sunny day. The roar of the helicopters was so loud that Randi stuck her fingers in her ears as the winds produced by the propellers tried to rip the hat off her head. They were gone as quickly as they'd arrived, but Randi still didn't feel safe. They'd flown over the museum for a reason. They'd be circling back soon.

Jake seemed to know it, too. He dug into his backpack and brought out a small hammer.

"I'm going to lower you down to the window right below us. Break the glass. Go inside and release the cord from your safety harness. You should be in the stairwell. The exhibit is one flight up. Don't hesitate, or you'll be captured before you make it to the eggs."

Randi nodded and took the hammer. The next five minutes were going to be among the most important of her life.

Within seconds, she was dangling back over the ground. Just as Jake had said, a window was right in front of her. She pulled back her arm and hit the glass. A long, thin crack grew from a tiny crater in the center of the window. But the glass didn't shatter. Another hit with the hammer, and a new crack appeared. Randi was growing desperate, but she couldn't afford to panic. Instead she cleared her mind, bent her knee, and kicked the window with a force she never imagined she could muster. The window caved in, and Randi was inside.

She dropped the hammer, released the cord to her safety

harness, and sprinted up the stairs. Randi could hear alarms wailing elsewhere in the building, but when she threw open the door to the fifth-floor exhibition space, the only sounds she heard were the tinkling of crystal glasses and a few notes of Tchaikovsky's *Swan Lake*.

As she'd suspected, the eggs were out of their cages. They were lined up on a long table covered with jet-black velvet. There was no barrier between the eggs and their admirers.

A woman shrieked at the sight of Randi, and a hundred people in ball gowns and tuxedos spun around to face the door to the stairwell.

"What is it?" a woman cried.

"What does it want?" her husband added in a voice just as shrill as his wife's.

"Please, settle down!" ordered a man in a calm, clear, and familiar voice. "There's no cause for concern. It's just a little girl with an overactive imagination."

It was Officer Cody, marching across the room, his hand already reaching for the handcuffs affixed to his belt loops. The guests backed up, as if Randi were a wild animal that might lunge at them at any second.

Randi couldn't let Officer Cody stop her. But she couldn't hurt him either. So she waited until he was close enough to grab. Then she took his hand, spun him around, and kicked the back of his knee just hard enough to make him lose his balance. The instant he was on the ground, Randi made her move.

She headed straight for the one egg she was certain was fake. Basket of Wild Flowers was a lovely white egg designed to resemble an Easter basket with a bouquet of flowers sprouting out of the top. The VIPs gasped in unison when Randi wrapped her fingers around the egg. Several people screamed—and a gentleman fainted—when Randi reared back her arm and threw it.

The egg shattered against a wall. Not just in two or three pieces but in thousands. Randi felt Officer Cody grab her by her harness. Her arms were bent backward and her wrists handcuffed.

"How could you do something so stupid?" he growled under his breath.

"Because you wouldn't have believed me otherwise," Randi said.

"Believed *what*?" the cop demanded.

"That some of these eggs aren't real. Think about it. A real egg wouldn't have shattered like that. The one I just threw was made out of *sugar*."

It took a minute for the information to sink in. Then the police officer dragged Randi along with him as he approached the remnants of the shattered egg. The crowd was clustered around the pile of shards, and a few people had bent over to examine them.

Officer Cody dropped into a squat and picked up the biggest piece he could find—a pink flower no bigger than a pearl.

He stuck the flower to his tongue and then hopped back to his feet.

"Everyone, stay right where you are!" he ordered. "This is officially a crime scene. I don't care if you're the Mayor of New York or the Duchess of Cambridge. Nobody leaves this room!"

But no one was listening. The sprinkler system had gone off. Women's hairdos were instantly flattened. Silk dresses and designer shoes were ruined. A man's toupee was washed right off his head. Dozens of guests rushed for cover. Some huddled in doorways. A few crawled beneath tables. Officer Cody watched the pandemonium, unsure of what to do next.

Randi tugged on his sleeve. "No one here stole the eggs," she told him. "The thieves are long gone. But if we act fast, you might be able to catch them."

"How many eggs did they get?" Officer Cody asked.

"We'll find out in a second," Randi told him.

The sprinklers shut off. By the time the sopping-wet guests emerged from their hiding places, the pedestals where six of the eggs had been sitting were empty. ☠

☠ Go to Appendix E to complete the Ninja Task!

CHAPTER SEVENTEEN

THE ART GALLERY

Officer Cody stepped into the interrogation room at the 78th Precinct in Brooklyn and held out one hand, its palm facing up. "Looks like we got the thieves," he announced.

After the torture she'd put her muscles through, Randi Rhodes could barely move her arms, but she still managed to give him five.

"Boris Usenko and Oleg Chudov, both well-known members of the Moscow crime scene. And Dieter Koch, a German pastry chef. Thanks to that luggage tag you dug out of the trash, we found out they were on an Aeroflot flight from JFK to Moscow. We reached the pilot before they left American airspace. The jet just landed in Portland, Maine."

"And the eggs?" Randi asked. "Have you found them yet?"

"The Feds took Andrei Gorchakov into custody a few hours ago. He had the eggs in his possession. They're on their way back to the museum as we speak, and Officer Jackson is searching for the location of Gorchakov's private art gallery."

"Tell him to try Gorchakov's wine cellar," Randi said suddenly.

She didn't even have to explain her hunch. Officer Cody took out his phone and dialed Officer Jackson's right away.

"Miranda says check the wine cellar. . . ." He paused and listened for a moment. "So what if it's the size of an Appalachian Outhouse? Try searching for a secret door or something. If she says it might be down there, it's worth another look."

Randi beamed. It felt good to be taken seriously.

"I heard Gorchakov mention his wine cellar at the Russian Tea Room," she explained once Officer Cody was off the phone. "He said he couldn't wait to rearrange it, which didn't seem to make any sense. . . ."

The door swung open and a female officer stuck her head into the room. "Sorry to interrupt. There's someone here for Miranda Rhodes," she said. "He says he's her dad."

Randi glared at Officer Cody. "I thought you promised you weren't going to call him."

The police officer held his hands up. "I didn't," he told her.

Suddenly Herb Rhodes was standing in the doorway. His shirt was untucked and his hair hadn't been brushed. Randi stood up, preparing for a lecture. Instead, she received a hug.

"Gigi called me," he said. "She told me everything. I hopped on a plane right away."

"Are you mad at me?" Randi asked.

Her dad cleared his throat. "I'm absolutely furious," he croaked, holding her even closer.

"Sir," Officer Cody said. "If it's any consolation, your daughter is a first-class detective. She just foiled one of the biggest heists in New York City history."

Officer Cody's phone rang before Herb Rhodes had a chance to respond. When the redheaded cop hung up, he was grinning from ear to ear.

"Looks like Miranda's accomplishments just got even more impressive," he said. "Thanks to her tip, my colleague just found Andrei Gorchakov's private art gallery. He says it's one of the most amazing things he's ever seen. Almost everything in it is stolen. How would you both like a look?"

Officer Jackson met them outside a modest brick house in a Russian neighborhood in Brooklyn. It looked like every other building on the block—two stories high with a cute white porch. Aside from the Rolls-Royce parked out front, there was absolutely nothing that would have suggested the house was home to a notorious gangster.

"Follow me," Officer Jackson said. "You're not going to believe this."

He guided them through several ordinary, if tastefully furnished, rooms to a plain wooden door in the kitchen on the house's first floor. Behind the door lay a set of stairs that led to an underground room.

"It's going to get a little tight down here for a moment," Officer Jackson informed them. He waited until his three guests had descended the stairs. At the bottom was a tiny room lined with wine racks.

"He's got some pretty good stuff here," Herb Rhodes said, pulling a bottle out for a closer look.

"Yep, but this one here's the best in his collection." Officer Jackson pointed at a dark green bottle with a burgundy cap. "See what you think."

Herb pulled at the bottle, but it wouldn't leave the rack. Randi heard a loud click, and the wall that held the rack began to move. A hidden entrance appeared before them. Randi took one step inside and gasped.

She'd expected a fancy basement. What she'd found instead was an underground palace. The room she was in was bigger than her entire house. Its white walls were trimmed with bright blue and gold. Gilded statues stood in every corner, and three crystal chandeliers hung from the ceiling. Plush sofas and armchairs were clustered around sumptuous Oriental carpets.

"There's an FBI agent around here somewhere," Officer Jackson said. "He says this is a copy of a room in a famous palace in Saint Petersburg, Russia. In fact, all the rooms down here are inspired by palaces once owned by the Russian royal family."

"Wait," Randi said. "What other rooms? There's more than this one down here?"

"Oh, this is just the start." Officer Jackson laughed. "Gorchakov must have burrowed under the entire borough of Brooklyn to build this place. But let me show you the best part." He walked over to a small painting that was hanging on the wall. It showed a dark vase filled with yellow and red flowers. "This is a van Gogh painting. It was stolen from a museum in Cairo in 2010. It's worth fifty-five million dollars."

"*Fifty*-five?" Herb Rhodes repeated.

"For a picture of some flowers?" Randi asked.

"That's right," said Officer Jackson. He moved on to the next painting on the wall. It showed a man and two women in old-fashioned clothing playing music. "And this one's by Johannes Vermeer. It was stolen from the Gardner Museum in Boston in 1990. It's worth around two hundred million dollars."

Herb Rhodes collapsed onto one of the sofas. "My daughter helped recover a two-hundred-million-dollar painting?"

"Oh, there's a lot more than that down here. I've been following the FBI's art expert around for the past hour. There are sculptures and paintings that no one has seen in decades. And at least one item that hasn't been seen in almost a century." Officer Jackson reached into his jacket pocket and pulled out an egg. It was a pale purplish pink. "The expert thinks this may be what's known as the Mauve Egg. It's been lost since the Russian Revolution in 1917. And all of the eggs that mysteriously vanished are down here as well."

"Looks like you're going to be famous," Officer Cody told Randi. "A twelve-year-old girl helped uncover a fortune in stolen art? The press is going to be all over you."

"*Oy*," said Herb Rhodes, sinking even further into the over-stuffed sofa. "If the press is all over her, this guy's mob buddies will be, too."

"And once they find out you're the daughter of a best-selling mystery writer . . . ," Officer Cody continued.

"You're going to be on TV for *weeks*," Officer Jackson finished.

The idea was appealing, but there was only one response Randi could give. "I'd rather not," she told the police officers.

"What?" Officer Cody blurted out.

"Why?" Officer Jackson asked.

"I don't want to be famous," Randi replied.

"You don't?" Herb Rhodes asked in astonishment.

"Of course not," Randi told him. "How am I supposed to have any fun if I'm being watched all the time?" ☠

☠ Go to Appendix F to complete the Ninja Task!

CHAPTER EIGHTEEN

PRICELESS OBJECTS

Monday morning, the three ninja detectives went their separate ways. D.C., Gigi, and Jake headed to Chinatown to film action scenes for *The Littlest Warrior*, Jake Jessop's latest martial arts film. Pudge stayed at Gigi's house to prepare for his dad's arrival later that afternoon. He'd finished a grueling workout routine and had already washed his laundry and was waiting for the iron to heat up when Randi and Herb Rhodes came in to say good-bye.

"You're going to iron all of your T-shirts and jeans?" Randi asked.

"Of course," Pudge replied. "They look better that way."

"What happened to the eat-what-you-want, sleep-in-your-clothes Pudge I've come to know and love?" Randi teased him.

"I was on *vacation*!" Pudge argued. "I don't want to live like that *forever*."

"So you're ready to go home, then?" Herb asked.

Pudge picked up the iron and began to smooth the wrinkles

out of a Boston Red Sox T-shirt. "I never thought I'd say this, but *yeah*. I've had enough craziness to last me a while. I can't wait to watch *The Little Mermaid* and eat a *whole lotta* broccoli. I just hope my dad never finds out about half the stuff I did here. If he ever heard I had five pieces of pie . . ."

"You think he doesn't know what you've been up to?" Herb Rhodes asked the boy.

Pudge looked up with a horrified expression. "Did someone tell him?"

"Why do you think he let you stay? He's a colonel now, but he was a twelve-year-old once, too. He knows that kids your age have to blow off some steam once in a while."

Pudge's relief was clear. "So he'll be okay with it?"

Herb Rhodes clapped a hand on Pudge's shoulder. "He met Gigi, didn't he? He knew what he was getting himself into. But I'm not sure I'd tell him about the pie. And not because it would make him mad. Five pieces of pie? I'm feeling sick just thinking about it!"

"That makes two of us," Pudge said.

On the subway, Herb Rhodes sat with a box in his lap. It was a plain, square cardboard box, about eight inches deep and eight inches wide. It was the perfect size to hold a small cake. But the way Herb handled the box with care, Randi suspected there was something far more precious inside.

They got out of the subway on Twenty-Fifth Street and

walked to Green-Wood Cemetery. The tall gates that guarded Brooklyn's largest graveyard look liked the entrance to a fairy tale kingdom, with their tall spires reaching up to the heavens. Squawking green parrots had made their nests in every nook and cranny of the brown stone structure.

Without a word passing between them, Randi and her father headed down a path that led up a hill, past the mausoleums of famous politicians, mobsters, artists, and actresses. In a peaceful valley, near a giant sassafras tree, they reached their destination. There, a simple granite tombstone read, *Olivia-Kay Daly Rhodes, 1972–2012.*

"Hi, Mom," Randi said, laying the flowers she had brought down on the grave. She and her father had gone to three different florists to find blue hydrangeas. They'd been her mother's favorite flower. "I've missed you so much."

Whatever greeting Herb Rhodes offered his wife, he didn't say it aloud. But he brushed her tombstone gently with the tips of his fingers. Then he lowered himself down to the ground. Once there, he patted the grass beside him.

"Sit down," he told Randi. "I have something to show you."

The ground was cold. Randi could feel a chill working its way up her spine.

"Are you going to tell me what's in the box now?" she asked. "Is it something for Mom?"

Herb Rhodes looked down at the parcel he'd been carrying. "No, Randi. It's for you. When we left Brooklyn last summer, I asked Gigi to store some things for me. There were a few items that your mom wanted you to have when you got older. And a couple of things that I was saving to show you."

"Why didn't you bring them to Deer Creek?" Randi asked.

"When you live with a girl detective," Herb Rhodes said, "it's hard to keep anything secret." He passed the package to his daughter. "You can open it now."

Randi took the lid off the box. Inside was a soft round nest made of twigs and straw. In its center was a brilliant blue egg that was twice as big as a chicken's egg and covered in delicate white morning glories.

"It's not as fancy as a Fabergé egg," Herb said. "But your mom wasn't the kind of lady who went for gemstones and diamonds. The things that fascinated her about Fabergé eggs were the secrets that they each held inside. She never missed an opportunity to get a close look at one. I can still remember how excited she was when that big exhibition came to the Frick thirteen years ago. It took her weeks to figure out how to get into the museum after hours."

Randi grinned. "So Mom really was the lady in black that Colonel Taylor caught breaking into the Frick—the one who called herself Glenn Street."

"Oh yes. Whenever your mom went on one of her adventures, she always used an alias, and Glenn Street was one of her favorites. She was the one who dreamed up the name. I wasn't even a writer in those days. At the time, I worked in a vacuum cleaner shop."

"Wow, that sounds really . . ."

"Dull?" Herb Rhodes finished the sentence for her. "Yep. I guess I was the boring one in the family back then. But your mom kept things exciting. She had a knack for finding adventure wherever she went. She'd take a quick trip to the grocery store and end up chasing down a thief who'd snatched an old lady's purse. Or she'd read about some mystery in the newspaper and spend weeks trying to solve it."

"She sounds like a lot of fun," Randi said.

"She sounds a lot like her daughter," Herb replied. "And Olivia-Kay *was* fun. But it could be a bit nerve-racking to love someone so wild. My worst fear was that one day she'd turn up some trouble she couldn't handle. I knew I wouldn't survive if anything had happened to Olivia-Kay."

"Did she know how worried you were?" Randi asked.

"Sure. I didn't try to hide it. But that was who Olivia-Kay was, and I didn't want to change her. I figured she'd keep chasing after adventure until she was too old to chase anything. Then one Easter morning, she gave me this." Herb Rhodes took the egg out of its nest and handed it to Randi. It was much lighter than she'd imagined. "Open it."

Randi pulled the two halves of the egg apart. A smaller egg lay inside. It was decorated with a miniature painting of a river with green mountains in the background. A group of tiny kids were jumping off of a wooden dock.

"Is that Deer Creek?" Randi asked. There was already a lump in her throat.

"Yep," Herb Rhodes said. "Olivia-Kay must have painted it with a magnifying glass. That scene shows the day that your mom and I met."

When Randi held the egg up for a closer look, she noticed a thin crack that circled the egg. "This one opens too?" When her dad nodded, she twisted the top of the egg. Inside was another, even tinier egg. Little blue flowers were affixed to its surface using a technique called decoupage.

"They're real," Herb Rhodes told her. "They were growing in the field where your mom and I got married. She must have picked some and pressed them. That egg opens as well."

It was so small that Randi couldn't imagine what might be inside. It opened lengthwise to reveal a tiny figure swaddled in an even tinier blanket.

"What is this?" Randi asked.

"That's you," Herb Rhodes said. "This egg was how your mom told me that we were having a baby."

Randi took the baby out of the egg and held it in her palm. It was about an inch and a half long, but perfect in every way— from the lock of red hair that peeked out from beneath its cap to the perfect little mouth that looked like it might be laughing.

"Your mom told me that the Frick was going to be her last big adventure for a while. I don't think she ever intended to give it all up for good. But once she had you, she wanted to make sure that she would always be there if you needed her. I was so touched by the sacrifice that I sat down that night and started writing the first Glenn Street book. If she couldn't have her adventures in real life, at least she could read about them on the page."

Randi tried to brush her tears away. "Dad, why didn't you . . . ?"

"I know I should have told you this earlier," he said. "I guess it was just too hard for me to talk about. You lost your mother, Randi, and I lost the love of my life."

Randi had often wondered if her father's true love had been Glenn Street. She'd imagined her mom having to compete with the character for her husband's attention. Now she realized that the two women had been one and the same.

"I know you think that I should have spent more time at home while your mom was alive," Herb continued. "And you're right. But you have to understand that Olivia-Kay was always with me—even when I was writing or away on a tour. She knew that, Randi. She knew that every book I wrote was a love letter to her."

Just like her dad's new book was a love letter to *her*, Randi realized. She wrapped her arms around her dad and squeezed him with all her might.

"There's something else," Herb said. "I spoke to your aunt. She told me that you're welcome to live in New York with her if you'd like. I moved us down to Deer Creek to be closer to your mom. I know her grave is here, but her spirit is down there. But I'm starting to realize that it might not have been the best thing for the two of us. I don't want you to feel like I'm holding you back. You're just like your mother, Randi. If I'd tried to control her, I would have ended up losing her. So I'm going to let you make this decision. What do you want to do?"

"I want to go home," Randi told him.

"Is home here in Brooklyn or in east Tennessee?"

"Home is wherever you are," Randi told her dad. ⚐

_____

⚐ Go to Appendix G to complete the Ninja Task!

CHAPTER NINETEEN

THE MOVIE STAR

"Can I have your autograph?" A pack of fourth graders had surrounded D.C., and one of them was holding out a small notebook and pen. The local television channel had just run a segment about D.C.'s role in the upcoming martial arts movie *The Littlest Warrior*, and the town of Deer Creek was buzzing with the news.

D.C. signed the first page of the notebook and handed it back to the kid.

"Mine too!" cried another boy.

"So how does it feel being a bona-fide movie star?" Randi asked D.C.

"Pretty darn good," the boy replied. "My dad even heard about it somehow. He called me last night to congratulate me."

"And you talked to him?" Randi asked. "After the way he behaved when you were in Brooklyn?"

"Sure," D.C. said with a shrug. "Jake says holding grudges is a waste of energy."

"Maybe Jake should have a word with Amber-Grace," Randi said. She'd spotted the bottle-blonde lurking in the hallway ahead. As always, her band of overdressed girls was by her side. "Looks like our absence hasn't made her heart grow any fonder."

There was no avoiding them. The girls were blocking the hall that led to Randi and D.C.'s next class. The bell rang and the kids surrounding D.C. scattered. Amber-Grace and her posse didn't budge.

"How about that? It's the motherless Yankee and her sissy friend," Amber-Grace sneered as they drew closer. "If you guys were smart, you'd have stayed in New York City."

"You're not welcome here in Tennessee," said one of her friends.

"Oh yeah?" D.C. asked. "Looks to me like you're the only ones in the school who feel that way."

"You sure about that? I heard that your own daddy doesn't even want you around, Dario Cruz," Amber-Grace said. "And your mama probably jumped off a bridge just to get away from you, Randi Rhodes."

Once, the mention of her mother's death would have left Randi reeling. But Amber-Grace's words couldn't wound her the way they used to.

"You know, Amber-Grace, you're going to get yourself into a whole lotta trouble talking like that," Randi said in a calm, clear voice.

"Oh yeah?" the older girl replied. "Does it make you feel like punching me? Come on, Yankee. Get yourself thrown out of school."

Randi looked over at D.C. and grinned. "Does it make you feel like punching her?"

"Nope," said D.C., playing along.

"Me either," Randi agreed. "But you know what it does make me feel like doing, D.C.? It makes me feel like keeping really close tabs on Amber-Grace here. If she insists on harassing us, we should probably get to know her a bit better. I've always wondered what sort of stuff she does after school. Or when she's out with her friends. Or on a date with Stevie. I think we should start keeping a file on her, don't you?"

"You're talking about spying on me?" Amber-Grace snarled.

"Oh man," D.C. chipped in, ignoring the girl. "I bet we'd come up with some *amazing* stuff."

"And we could take pictures and film videos of her being nasty to people," Randi added. "And put them on the Internet so her parents and everyone at school could enjoy them."

"You wouldn't dare," Amber-Grace spat.

"Oh, I would," Randi assured her. She pulled out her cell phone. "In fact, I've already started. This whole conversation has been recorded. I can think of a few people who might find it very interesting, can't you, D.C.?"

"Yup," D.C. said. "Should we post it on Facebook?"

"You wouldn't dare!" Amber-Grace darted forward to smack the phone out of Randi's hand. But D.C.'s reflexes were lightning fast. He caught the girl's wrist and held it tight.

"Careful, Amber-Grace," Randi warned. "I hear this school has a zero-tolerance policy when it comes to violence."

D.C. let the girl go, and Randi held up her phone. "You're on video now. Anything you'd like to say for the camera?"

Amber-Grace hid her face with one hand. Her friends followed suit. "This isn't over," Amber-Grace growled through her fingers. "Let's go, girls," she ordered, and she and her posse stomped off down the hall.

"Nice work," D.C. told Randi.

"You too. For a moment there, I was worried we might need backup. And speaking of backup, where's Pudge?" Randi asked.

"Skipping school," D.C. told her. "He went fishing with his dad. But he said he and his sisters will be at your house for the premiere tonight."

For a moment, it felt like the entire world had been turned upside down. "Colonel Taylor took Pudge fishing on a school day?"

"Yup," said D.C. "I guess Pudge had his hands full with those three girls on the ride back from New York. The colonel told Pudge that they needed to spend more time together alone."

"Wow," Randi said. "Who'd have thought it would take only

one long weekend to turn you into a movie star and Pudge into a hooky-playing delinquent?"

"And what about you?" D.C. asked with a laugh.

"Me?" Randi said innocently. "I'm just an ordinary Deer Creek kid."

That night, eleven people took their seats in the Rhodeses' living room to enjoy a feast and a movie. Jake Jessop had sent tapes of D.C.'s scenes in *The Littlest Warrior*. And Mei-Ling, Herb Rhodes, and Mrs. Taylor had fried up the fish that Pudge and his father had caught.

"So when do we get to watch your whole film?" Colonel Taylor asked D.C.

"Yeah, when?" Maya and Laeleah chimed in. Pudge's twin sisters had become D.C.'s biggest fans.

"Jake said it should be done before Christmas," D.C. told them.

"He and Gigi promised to bring a copy when they come to visit for New Year's," Herb Rhodes added.

"I can't wait to meet them," D.C.'s mother said. She grabbed D.C. and pulled her son into a hug. "And I don't even know how I'll possibly thank them."

"Whatever you do, don't bake a pie," Pudge said with a queasy look on his face.

Randi laughed and dropped onto the couch next to Mei-Ling.

The older woman wrapped her arm around Randi and squeezed. "Does this mean you're back for good?" she whispered.

Randi put her head on Mei-Ling's shoulder. "There's nowhere I'd rather be," Randi told her.

NINJA TASKS

Now that you've helped to solve another mystery, you can try all these experiments at home. Find a partner—recruit Mom and Dad, Gram or Gramps, or invite your best friend over. Follow the evidence and enjoy the fun!

DISAPPEAR IN THE DARK

Things You'll Need:
- Dark—not black—clothing
- Soft-soled shoes
- Patience

What to Do:
» **CHOOSE** your clothing carefully. Black clothing isn't ideal for hiding in the dark—and it could make you seem suspicious. A dark gray sweat suit may be the best option. Not only will it allow you to hide in the shadows, but if you're caught, you can always claim you were out for a jog.

» **CAMOUFLAGE** yourself when possible. No one ever looks twice at a pile of leaves.

» **WEAR** soft-soled shoes. The more you can feel the soles of your feet, the easier it will be to avoid making noise as you walk.

» **HONE** your night vision. Spend twenty minutes allowing your eyes to get used to the dark. And when you leave, don't bring your phone! One look at the screen can ruin your night vision.

» **STAY** as still as possible. The human eye is very sensitive to movement. The less you move, the less likely you are to be seen. If you can't stay still, stay low to the ground.

» **PLAN** a diversion in advance. In case you're about to be spotted, have a plan that will draw attention away from you.

» **PRACTICE** moving silently and "vanishing." Try sneaking up on your parents—or watching your siblings from the shadows.

Go Incognito

Things You'll Need:

- Rubber band
- Hat
- Scarf or sweater
- Glasses
- Cotton balls

What to Do:

» **CHANGE** your hairstyle for a quick and easy transformation. Even something as simple as putting your hair into a ponytail—or covering it up with a hat—can make a big difference in the way you look. Of course, if you have a wig at your disposal, feel free to make use of it. (As long as it's not brightly colored or oddly styled.)

» **ALTER** your clothing. If you're a girl, a scarf may be the best accessory you'll ever own. A single scarf can change your outfit in a dozen ways. But if scarfs aren't an option, layer your clothing (sweater over shirt over T-shirt). Stripping off a layer—or adding one on—can make it look like you're wearing a totally different outfit.

» **ALWAYS** carry a pair of glasses. It's the simplest way to keep people from recognizing you. Stuffing your cheeks with a few cotton balls can also change the shape of your face—not to mention the sound of your voice.

» **DON'T** call attention to yourself. Wear drab clothing in bland colors. Avoid heavy makeup or fancy hairstyles. If possible, don't look anyone in the eye.

APPENDIX C:

Eat Some Flowers

Things You'll Need:

- Rose petals—or any other edible flower (violets, violas, pansies, etc.). Be sure to ask if a flower is edible before you eat it! And never use flowers that may have been sprayed with pesticides.
- One egg white
- Superfine sugar
- Pastry brush
- Wax paper

What to Do:

» **CLEAN** the petals and allow them to dry completely. If crystalizing whole flowers, be sure to remove the stems.

» **BEAT** the egg white. Using the pastry brush, cover each petal/flower with egg white.

» **SPRINKLE** both sides of the petals/flowers with superfine sugar and place on the wax paper.

» **ALLOW** the candied rose petals to dry overnight.

» **ENJOY!** Not only do candied flowers taste great and make fabulous decorations, but they're a delicious way to freak out your friends.

OPEN A LOCKED DOOR

Things You'll Need:

- A locked door in your own house
- A plastic card (an old credit card, school ID, or library card should do)
- That's it!

What to Do:

» **TAKE** your old card and insert it into the crack between the door and the frame—about two inches above the door handle.

» **SLIDE** the card down until it meets resistance. This is the lock catch.

» **GENTLY** push on the catch with the card until it gives. When the catch gives, the lock will open.

» **NEVER** break into another person's house. And now that you know how easy it can be to open a locked door, never forget to lock your dead bolt when you leave home!

Put Smashed Eggs to Good Use

Things You'll Need:

- Eggshells
- Flour
- Food coloring
- Waxed paper
- Tape
- Hot water

What to Do:

» **WASH** your eggshells well and set aside to dry.

» **POUND** the dry eggshells into a fine powder.

» **MIX** one teaspoon of eggshell powder with a teaspoon of flour and a teaspoon of hot water.

» **ADD** a few drops of food coloring and mix again. The result should be a firm paste.

» **FORM** the paste into the shape of a piece of chalk. Roll the chalk in wax paper and secure with a piece of tape.

» **REPEAT** the process using different shades of food coloring.

» **ALLOW** the paste to dry for three or four days. Unwrap the wax paper and discover . . . sidewalk chalk!

MAKE YOUR OWN SUGAR SCULPTURES

Things You'll Need:

- Adult supervision
- Hard candy (like Jolly Ranchers) in multiple colors
- Plastic sandwich bags
- A hammer
- Metal cookie cutters in cool shapes (skulls, ninjas, zombies)
- A nonstick cookie sheet
- An oven

What to Do:

» **HEAT** your oven to 325° degrees.

» **PLACE** unwrapped candies inside the plastic bags, keeping the colors separate.

» **SMASH** the candies into shards, using the hammer. (Watch your fingers!)

» **PUT** your cookie cutters onto the cookie sheet and fill each one with candy pieces.

» **BAKE** the candies for ten minutes. Allow five minutes to cool.
Then pop out your sugar sculptures!

Send a Secret Message in an Egg

Things You'll Need:

- An ordinary egg (raw with shell)
- A needle
- Paper and pen
- Glue that dries white
- Paint (optional)

What to Do:

» **TAKE** the needle and use it to carefully drill two little holes in the eggshell—one on each end.

» **PUT** your lips to one of the holes and blow. The raw egg inside the shell will be forced out the hole on the opposite end of the egg. (Unless you want to make a huge mess, blow it into a sink or bowl!) Continue to blow until the eggshell is completely empty.

» **RINSE** the empty eggshell well and set it aside to dry (inside and outside).

» **CUT** a small strip of paper. Write your secret message on the paper, and then roll the strip up tightly.

» **INSERT** the paper into the empty eggshell (once the shell has had time to dry).

» **COVER** the holes in the eggshell with little dollops of glue, then smooth. Allow time to dry.

» **PAINT** your creation if it's Easter (or if you're feeling fancy). Otherwise, let your secret message delivery system go undercover as an ordinary egg! Your note will remain hidden until someone cracks open the egg and finds it!